THE DOCTOR'S SECRET CHILD

KATE WELSH

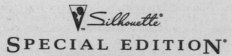

SPECIAL EDITION®

Published by Silhouette Books

America's Publisher of Contemporary Romance

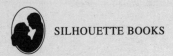 SILHOUETTE BOOKS

ISBN 0-373-24734-6

THE DOCTOR'S SECRET CHILD

Copyright © 2006 by Kate Welsh

Visit Silhouette Books at www.eHarlequin.com

Printed in U.S.A.

Books by Kate Welsh

Silhouette Special Edition

The Doctor's Secret Child #1734

Love Inspired

KATE WELSH

is a two-time winner of Romance Writers of America's coveted Golden Heart® and was a finalist for RWA's RITA® Award in 1999. Kate lives in Havertown, Pennsylvania, with her husband of over thirty years. When not at work in her home office creating stories and the characters that populate them, Kate fills her time in other creative outlets. There are few crafts she hasn't tried at least once or a sewing project that hasn't been a delicious temptation. Those ideas she can't resist grace her home or those of friends and family.

As a child she often lost herself in creating make-believe worlds and happily-ever-after tales. Kate turned back to creating happy endings when her husband challenged her to write down the stories in her head.

To Andy and Paul. Thanks for all the years of friendship and encouragement you've given me in my writing and all the love and support you've selflessly given both of us through these last difficult years.

Prologue

From the library window of the Hopewell Manor Caroline Hopewell watched the swollen river that flowed behind the property. She inhaled deeply, searching for calm in the powdery scent of the baby in her arms and the lemon-oil smell of the recently polished bookshelves surrounding her. There was a faint mustiness, too, from the myriad books stacked on the cherry floor-to-ceiling shelves that lined the room's walls. Some of those precious books had been in this room for over a hundred years.

The familiar room did nothing to calm her thoughts. Her emotions were as tangled as the clumps of plant material tumbling along in the river's flow and as murky and clouded as the muddy water itself. Now, after the reading of her father's will, she knew what they'd suspected for days—the seventeenth-century home and the extensive grounds surrounding it would be James Hopewell's only legacy.

His only decent one, at any rate. He'd certainly left plenty of scandal behind for them all to live down.

Caroline pushed that thought to the back of her mind, but then her thoughts drifted to the reason there had been a reading of her father's will at all.

James Gallagher Hopewell was dead. Even with all the bitterness she felt toward her father, Caro did grieve. And she knew her mother grieved, too. Not necessarily for the man who'd died but for the one she'd married twenty-three years ago.

Still, Caroline felt like a fool for missing the man after the way he'd deserted her wonderful mother and married a much younger woman who was pregnant with his child. She cuddled that sweet baby against her shoulder now, loving her brother despite all the bitterness and anguish that had surrounded his birth.

One question haunted Caroline about her father's death and the last time she'd seen him. Had he sensed that his trip was doomed? She would never forget the look in his eyes when he'd handed Jamie to her and asked her to take care of his son if anything happened to them. She'd been just the tiniest bit angry at the time. It was Christmas, after all. Jamie's first. And they were leaving their baby behind to go off for a holiday with clients. She'd rashly taken the baby from him and made her empty promise.

Turning, she faced her mother. At forty, Juliana Hopewell was still a beautiful, spirited woman. Her strawberry-blond hair was still as shining and vibrant as her bright green eyes. Everyone said they looked alike except for their hair color. Her own was more golden than her mother's. They had the same high cheekbones, slightly squared jawline and full lips. Even the accentuated tilt of their eyes and the brows that arched over them were similar.

"Come, Caro. Tell me," her mother said, gesturing to the chair across from her. The matching wingback chairs sat nestled next to the warm glow of the firelight that valiantly fought back the gloom.

Caro walked across the room and glanced down at the intricate pattern of the antique Persian carpet, praying her decision didn't add to her mother's pain. Didn't ruin her own life. Or Jamie's.

You've got no choice, she told herself. *You promised.* It had been an empty one at the time, but it was no longer. "Mama? I've made a decision I hope you can understand." Even Caroline heard the plea in her own voice.

Juliana's troubled thoughts were easy for Caro to read, maybe because they were as alike in temperament as appearance. So much had changed in so little time. "Do you really think I don't know what you're going to say?" her mother asked.

Caroline rubbed Jamie's back in an effort to keep the ten-month-old calm and took a deep breath, hoping she'd sound strong and resolute. "I want to keep Jamie with me if the court will let me. And eventually I'm going to try to adopt him. If Natalie had had family, I'd have to think about letting them raise him, but she didn't. And I can't just let the state place him with strangers, Mama. He should grow up here. I know it isn't fair to you. None of this has been fair to you. And now…"

"Sit. You've been walking him for hours."

Caroline sat and huffed out a tired breath, then sank deeply into the leather wingback chair the fire had already warmed for her in welcome. She heard the acceptance in her mother's voice, but it was edged with pain. Pushing back the hair that had slipped onto her face, Caro glanced at her mother, wanting to erase the hurt that had filled the past year. Her father's affair, the divorce, the baby, the accident and now even in death her father had burdened her mother with his will. She still wasn't sure if it had been good or bad news. "You looked surprised that Father made you trustee of Hopewell."

Her mother's perfectly arched eyebrows rose. "I'm still a little surprised."

"I don't think it was fair," Caro said honestly. You weren't supposed to speak ill of the dead, but she hated unfairness. And it seemed her father hadn't known how to be fair. "I know you. Now you're going to feel obligated to make ends meet around here," she went on. He'd left both of them feeling obligated.

Juliana nodded, her hands busily ordering the stack of magazines that had slipped in her lap. "I prefer to think, in his way, James was *trying* to be fair."

"But it ties you to this place."

"Caro, your father knew I love this majestic old pile of stone and brick as much as he did. He knew I'd take care of it until his children could. The will gives me a life lease on the house in exchange for keeping it safe for his children. He loved you all very much. He—" Juliana paused and dropped the magazines into the rack next to her chair. "He was the best father he knew how to be."

"And an undeniably lousy husband," Caroline countered.

"Water under the bridge. Hopewell belongs to you and your sisters and brother now. Your father and Natalie are gone. Which brings us to this decision of yours. A baby is a burden, Caro. Especially Jamie. Do you think I don't hear him crying all the time?"

Caroline stiffened. "His parents are dead. He's just unsettled."

"What was the excuse before they died? He cries at the least little thing. I know you love your brother. I do, too. You know I'd never take the things James and Natalie did out on Jamie."

Caro did know that. It was one of the reasons she felt she could make the decision. Her mother did love Jamie in spite of his parentage. "I can't give him to strangers."

"I know. But your life is just beginning."

Caroline's eyes misted with tears. She found herself holding the baby just a bit tighter. She laid her cheek on his downy head, feeling so much more than obligation. "I can do this, Mama."

Juliana Hopewell smiled kindly, her green eyes full of gentle understanding. "That isn't in doubt. How hard it will be on you, however, and how much you'll have to give up because you're so intent on this is the issue." Her mother bit her lip as if about to say something difficult. "I've been thinking. I'll raise Jamie. As I said, I have a life lease here. And this is Jamie's home, too. I'm only forty. A lot of women these days are just beginning their families at my age."

"No!" She couldn't let this happen. "I promised him, Mama, and you raised your children. Abby's just started college. It's time for you to live for yourself for a change."

"And you have your whole life ahead of you," Juliana argued. "Believe me, most men don't want a ready-made family, no matter how pretty a bride you'd be. A child will change all your options."

Caroline looked down at the baby, then back up at her mother, her mind even more set on this course than before. "To be honest, Mama, I don't know that I'll ever marry after seeing what Father did to you. At least this way I'll have a child."

Juliana's voice rose with her fervor. "Marriage isn't just about children. It's about sharing laughter and tears with someone. It's about having someone to lean on."

Caro shook her head. "This is about more than what Father did. Remember Kyle? My so-called fiancé? The guy who said he loved me one day and then asked for his engagement ring back the next?"

"Kyle Winston was a social-climbing piranha and better out of your life. He wasn't a man. He was a weasel and he got what he deserved with that wife of his!"

Thinking of the way Kyle had looked the last time she'd seen him in town, with his arm full of packages, being pecked at by his wife, Caroline grinned. Her mother had a point, but he'd made her feel like such a fool! She'd seen it time and time again in the lives of her friends. Love made fools of otherwise intelligent people. It made a mess of their perfectly orderly lives. Look at the mess her father caused when he'd fallen in love with someone other than his wife!

Her mother continued, "Anyway, it's foolish to judge all men by the mistakes of two."

They would have to agree to disagree, Caro thought, but said, "We were talking about Jamie. If having him around all the time will be too painful, I'll get my own place as soon as I have a job."

Her mother looked horrified. "You will not! Having Jamie here is a reminder, yes, but the divorce wasn't all bad."

Caroline frowned. "I don't understand."

"All these years I thought I was happy. But I wasn't, and it was James's defection that showed me the truth. Now I'm finding out who I am and who I want to be."

"Who, Mama?"

Juliana hesitated. "Promise you won't think I've gone around the bend?"

Caro arched an eyebrow. "You are the most level-headed person I've ever met. Who do you want to be?"

Her mother grimaced but went on. "Not who. What. My settlement won't last forever. I don't have a career and, as you said, I have a long life ahead of me. I have to support myself, as do all of you. I've been thinking about that a lot."

"Thinking's good," Caroline said, smiling encouragingly.

"I want to move ahead with my plans for that land up on the bluff that I bought with part of my divorce settlement."

"I thought you bought it because it always reminded you of Italy," Caro said, holding her mother's gaze.

"It does remind me of Italy and the vineyard where I grew up. It takes me back to a simpler time, so I go there to think. I sit on the porch of that lovely crumbling Victorian and dream. I want to grow grapes on the hillsides and build a winery, Caro. We could open it to the public for wine tasting and have catered events in the beautiful setting we create." Juliana's eyes, green as her own, fairly sparkled with glee. "And we could convert that big old house into a bed-and-breakfast. It would overlook row after row of vines," she went on dreamily. "Eventually we could add a banquet facility. What do you think?"

Caroline felt her mother's excitement burst to life within her. "I could keep Jamie with me instead of putting him in day care and use my business degree to run the business end. Sammy could learn about growing the grapes, since she's going to agriculture school already. She'd love that! And Abby always talks about hotel management and event planning. Oh, and Mama, you could learn to be a vintner the way you'd started to before you married Father."

"That's exactly what I thought. I'll finally be a vintner."

Caroline's laugh startled the baby in her arms. "Great minds think alike. What shall we call it?"

Juliana grinned. "Hopewell Vineyard, of course."

Chapter One

Six years later

"It's Mother," a disembodied voice from the answering machine resounded inside Trey Westerly's aching head as he walked into his apartment. "Did you hear me, Wesley? Where is that doorman?"

Probably hiding, Trey thought with a grimace and dropped his briefcase on a nearby chair. Everyone called him either "Trey" or "Doctor" if they wanted an answer. Everyone but his mother when she was in a managing mood. He groaned inwardly. He really wasn't in the mood to deal with a mission that included him, as this one obviously did.

Like the dutiful son he tried so hard to be, Trey sighed and lifted the receiver. "I assume you'd like to come up?" he asked. While waiting for an answer, he tucked the phone between his ear and shoulder to loosen his tie.

"Of course I want to come up. I missed you by minutes at the hospital. Consequently I had to take a cab here right after taking one there."

He ground his teeth. He'd just put in a sixteen-hour day. How inconsiderate of him to leave the office at nine o'clock at night when his mother might return early from a trip and show up unannounced to see him. Trey stabbed out the code to buzz her inside the lobby, then hung up the phone. He loved his mother. He really did. But sometimes he wished he were an orphan.

She could be a bit much at the end of a long day. If he counted the time spent in the four surgeries he'd performed that day, he'd been on his feet fourteen of those sixteen hours. He'd eaten his lunch reading X-rays. Because it was his housekeeper's night out, he'd eaten his dinner in an elevator on his way to saving the life of a gangbanger—a teen who'd probably be back on his table within a year or two. Sometimes he wondered why he did what he did.

Then he remembered the four-year-old with the internal injuries whose life he'd saved at five that morning. He remembered the tears of joy her grateful parents had shed when he'd told them she'd be fine. He remembered the smile the little girl had given him just before he'd left the hospital for the day. That was why he'd become a trauma surgeon.

Because they needed him. Even the gangbangers.

His mother's impatient knock dragged Trey back to the present. His head felt just a little better as he opened the door. He smiled as she barreled past him into the foyer. He was confident that his mother always meant well even if she resembled a five-foot-two-inch steamroller at times.

"Hello, Mother," he said. "To what do I owe this unprecedented late-night visit?" Trey followed and bent to kiss her on the cheek.

His question was met with silence. Which was even more unprecedented than a late-night visit. Trey stepped back and read uncertainty and deep turmoil in her eyes. Her faded blond hair was pinned up, but several strands had come loose from their moorings. Worse, her dress wasn't precisely pressed. He hadn't seen her this undone since he'd been a boy. This must be serious. "Mother? You look exhausted. And upset. What is it?"

Her hand fluttered to her creased brow. "I drove straight here from West Chester, then I got a cab to the hospital, then another here when you weren't there, as I said." She took a deep shuddering breath. "Perhaps if we sat for a moment."

"Of course." He gestured toward the long white sofa that dominated the living room. It faced the glass doors to the rooftop terrace that overlooked Central Park. She preceded him into the living room area and put her handbag on the glass table in front of her.

Trey settled in one of the comfortable club chairs across from her and watched with growing concern as she reached again for her silver-gray bag. After pulling it onto her lap, she worried at the catch. When she said nothing, he prodded, "So you were visiting Aunt Elaine?"

"No. Not Elaine. It was Helen Jeffers I went to see. West Chester, *Pennsylvania*. I was supposed to stay till the end of the week, but when I saw it, I had to come back to tell you. But of course I couldn't just tell you. Not over the phone. That just wouldn't have been right. Or kind. And besides that, you needed to actually see it. See *him*. You understand?"

Trey blinked. "No. Not at all." He wasn't sure if his mother was being too cryptic or if his headache had scrambled a perfectly reasonable message. "See who, Mother?"

"Oh. I suppose you don't see at all." Finally she stopped fumbling with the catch and straightened her shoulders. Suddenly decisive, she opened the purse and handed him a folded piece of newsprint. "When I think I might not have seen it at all… It's a miracle. Just a miracle. I went to visit Helen when I haven't gone to her home for nearly eight years. There was no reason for me to visit her there after you moved back home to New York, now was there? Helen adores Broadway, you see?"

Trey could only stare at her. He longed to say something light like, *Who are you and what have you done with my perfectly reasonable mother?* but Marilyn Guilford wasn't known for her easy wit, especially when she was this tense.

"Don't just sit there, Wesley. Look at it!" she scolded.

Once again Trey winced at the sound of his given name. His father was called Wes. His grandfather had snatched up Lee as a moniker years earlier. At about age twelve, with all the common derivatives already taken, he'd begun to insist on being called Trey. Thank God it took because it stopped a lot of persecution when he entered high school. What he'd never understood was if the previous owners of the name had hated it as much as he did, why pass on the misery to their progeny?

"It's Trey, Mother. Please." He squeezed the bridge of his nose, preparing to suffer further by focusing on the article. He read the headline. And instantly wondered why he should be expected to care about the family of the man who destroyed what was left of his marriage over seven years ago. Then he noticed the youngest member of the family sharing an oversize pair of scissors with the oldest member.

He blinked, sure his eyes were playing tricks.

And his heart stuttered in his chest.

His world tilted on its axis.

Was this some sort of elaborate April Fools' joke? He glanced back up at his mother. No. She wasn't that good an actress, nor did a practical joke of this magnitude fit her personality. He looked back down at the clipping and read the caption aloud just to ground himself in the world as he knew it—or as it had been until a second before. "Youngest Hopewell helps cut ribbon." And then he went on reading into the body of the article, seeking a reasonable explanation but finding the only one there could be. "Jamie Hopewell, adopted son of Caroline Hopewell and the youngest member of Bucks County's newest winemaking family, helped cut the ribbon on Bella Villa, their new banquet facility opening Saturday…." He trailed off as the truth behind the lies roared through his stunned mind.

Natalie had lied.

News of his ex-wife Natalie's marriage to James Hopewell had reached him through his mother's friend, Helen Jeffers, as had news of Natalie's death along with the death of her second husband a year later. That must have been six years ago.

So since then Caroline Hopewell must have adopted the boy. The boy who was a dead ringer for himself at that age.

The boy who had to be his son.

"Natalie lied," he said aloud this time. She hadn't been pregnant with Hopewell's child when they'd divorced but with his. He had a seven-year-old son he'd never known existed.

The question was, what was he going to do about it? What did he want to do?

It took Trey an hour to get rid of his mother and all her advice and twenty-four hours to make his decision. He weighed his options and obligations. His wants and the boy's needs. As much as he wished he could, he found he couldn't just forget about Jamie. As soon as he'd made a decision to try to become a part of his son's life, the course of several lives had changed. His and his son's and the life of the woman the boy apparently called Mother. Then Trey faced the difficult truth. No matter what he did, someone would be hurt.

Hoping to minimize any injuries, he decided to tread carefully. He'd see what he could find out firsthand, observe what he could, then proceed from there. It took two more days to arrange time off and for a detective to get him some very basic information on the situation and for his mother to make a reservation for him under her name at Cliff Walk Bed-and-Breakfast. Then, having carefully taken care of the arrangements, he drove down to Hopetown to learn about the life his son lived.

As he tooled along through the Pennsylvania countryside, Trey began to take note of his surroundings. The trees had begun to thicken with new growth. The canal and river flowed swiftly next to the winding road to Hopetown. And the town that took its name from Caroline Hopewell's seventeenth-century ancestor was abuzz with the promise of a brisk tourist season.

After leaving the town behind, he came upon Hopewell Manor. It was an elegant brick-and-stone colonial house with several brick outbuildings. The compound lay on a wide tract between the main road through Hopetown and the river. A sign marked the drive as private and proclaimed the estate's name. He slowed and read, "Hopewell Manor 1689. Josiah Hopewell built a crude log cabin on this tract in the fall of 1689 and began construction of the original section of the present manor house in March of 1690. Additions were made in 1756 and 1810." Another sign read, "Home of Josiah Hopewell, founder of Hopetown, PA. Born in 1659 in London. Died here in 1709."

"And Mother thinks our family has a long lineage in this country," he muttered, shaking his head. Trey turned his eyes back to the road, surmising that the winery and bed-and-breakfast must be on another piece of land. Anxious to have the coming meeting over, he continued his ride along the meandering road for about a mile and a half.

A wooden sign posted off to the left next to a steep drive proclaimed Hopewell Vineyard and Winery. Cliff

Walk Bed-and-Breakfast. Bella Villa Banquet Halls. The date below revealed that the vineyard had been in business for six years. The cracked granite drive led to the cliff above.

His nerves crackled as he drove on, shifting through all his gears to accommodate the arduous climb to the top of the cliff. He'd no sooner crested the top of the hill when a small boy, ears plugged into a portable CD player, tripped by the side of the drive. He watched with disbelief as the child picked himself up and without looking left or right ran in front of Trey's car in his rush to catch up to a man who was striding ahead of him.

Trey slammed on his brakes and, shaken, watched in shock as the boy ran on, calling to the man, who finally turned and waited for the reckless, bouncing child. Then, rather than correct the child for running in front of a car, as Trey was sure his squealing brakes must have announced, the man put his hands on the boy's shoulders and held him in place by pressing downward. "Settle down," he heard the man admonish the boy. "You don't want to go running among the vines and chance breaking one, do you?"

The vines? The child could have been killed and this guy was worried about the vines? How many times a day might this boy be placed in danger from visiting tourists and their cars? And this man never mentioned a need for caution near the drive or that the boy had just nearly been hit by a car.

And the boy wasn't just any boy. That wild-looking little urchin was surely Trey's own son.

Trey watched, and the longing ache in his soul that had begun when he'd learned of Jamie grew by leaps and bounds. Boy and man moved away toward a row of vines and the man began to perform some task with the plants. Jamie, seemingly eager to please, dug things from the canvas sack and handed them over.

The two were too far away then for Trey to tell exactly what they were doing, but it bothered him to see his son working alongside a common laborer. He didn't think there was a moment in his life when he'd been as dirty and ill-kept as his son was at that moment. Thank heaven he'd decided to show up unannounced or he'd never have learned of the life his child was forced to lead. Trey glanced at his watch. Why wasn't a seven-year-old in school, where he belonged?

Suddenly he had to call everything he'd supposed about Caroline Hopewell's motives into question. Why would a twenty-two-year-old young woman adopt her half brother and take on all the financial and emotional responsibility of raising a child not hers? Could there be some sort of inheritance behind the adoption? Or had she perhaps kept his son to punish him for the transgressions of his parents?

Needing to get on with his fact-finding mission, Trey dragged his gaze off the sad little tableau and followed the signs to Cliff Walk. The dark-haired, doe-eyed young woman at the tall mahogany registration desk in the corner of the foyer seemed distracted. She apparently didn't recognize his name when he signed the register, which was a relief. He needed time to look around and get the lay of the land before the family realized who he was.

After putting his bag in his room, Trey decided to take a tour of the vineyard. His lawyer had already warned him not to approach Jamie on his own, and he hadn't even considered it, but he was more than tempted now.

Juliana Hopewell was an elegant woman in her forties whom he thought he remembered from her picture in the paper with Jamie. She conducted the barrel tour of the winery and, as with the dark-haired woman who'd greeted him at the bed-and-breakfast, she seemed not to connect him with Natalie.

The wine operation appeared, at least on the surface, to be well run and moderately successful. Deep caves had been honed from the natural limestone, and though some of the wine was aged in traditional barrels, Hopewell Winery had apparently had some success in experimentally aging several of their wines in steel containers. After tasting the wines, Trey had to admit that the winery had a good future. Which meant he wouldn't need to worry about Jamie's material needs. But then again, money was the least of his worries.

Those worries increased when he doubled back through the bottling room as a shortcut back to Caroline Hopewell's office. He walked in on Juliana Hopewell in a hot and heavy clinch with a man. The man in question was Will Reiger, the person he'd seen Jamie working with among the vines earlier.

Trey turned to go, not wanting to call attention to himself by interrupting, when Jamie ran into the big room through another door and gasped. "Grandmom? Uncle Will, what are you doing to my grandmom?" he demanded, the conduct of both the adults clearly outside his ken.

The two sprang apart. Juliana Hopewell looked horrified. Will Reiger, the man he'd learned on the tour was the vineyard's head vintner, looked concerned for Jamie but he also looked a bit smug.

"I was giving her a great big hug," he told Jamie. "You want a great big hug? Sometimes people like hugs."

"You have to catch me," Jamie said as he whirled away and ran back out the door.

"You shouldn't have done that," Juliana snapped.

Reiger grinned. "Which? Kiss you or ask if he wanted a hug?"

"Both, damn you. Now go find Jamie and make sure he doesn't tell anyone else about what he saw. I don't want the girls getting foolish ideas about us."

"Maybe those ideas aren't foolish at all. And the *girls* are adult women. Maybe if their mother gave men a try again they might not think we're only around to do the heavy lifting."

Trey backed away then as the two stared at one another, their attention fixed. Rather than go to Caroline Hopewell's office, Trey walked in the other direction. He needed to clear his thoughts. Make some decisions. He didn't want to start out on the wrong foot with Jamie's adoptive mother. He had to keep fighting the urge to be angry with her. And most of all he had to keep himself from processing everything he saw through the filter of that anger. He also wondered if he should mention what Jamie had seen in the barrel room.

The day was warm, cloudless and sunny, and smelled of spring. The trees had begun to sprout green leaves, and tufts of grass dotted the landscape, blowing in a stiff breeze. There was a sweet smell on the wind, reminding Trey of what he missed by living in Manhattan, even if he was across the street from Central Park. But he acknowledged that he could hardly live in a quiet country setting like this. It was in the cities where trauma surgeons were needed most. After half an hour Trey gave up trying to sort through his angry thoughts. But no amount of walking seemed to help his troubled spirit. It all kept coming back to the very real fact that he'd lost seven years with his son—years Caroline Hopewell had had.

As if to reinforce his anguish over the whole situation, when he was on his way back to his room, Trey saw Reiger off in the distance. The man pelted along, his head turning this way and that as if he were searching for something. His movements quickly became more and more frantic as time marched along.

Was the vintner in search of Jamie?

Curious and concerned, Trey changed direction. When he got closer, Trey heard that the man was indeed calling for Jamie. His heart rate took off at a speed to match his now-racing feet. Trey had almost reached the vintner when he caught sight of something that nearly stopped his heart. Jamie had climbed high up in a pine tree that clung to an outcropping of rocks protruding out over a drop of several hundred feet to the rocky riverbank below.

Trey froze in place, as did Will Reiger when his gaze followed Trey's and lit on the figure high in the trees. Reiger cursed and both of them changed direction, jogging to the edge of the cliff.

"Jamie, boy. Come down from there," Reiger said in a quiet but commanding tone.

The boy straddled a branch, raised his face to the

wind and held his arms out as if to catch the air. "I can see clear to Hopetown, Uncle Will."

His heart in his throat, Trey asked, "What would possess him to climb so high? Should one of us go up after him?"

"Climbing up after him might not be such a good idea. He just might go higher. Jamie can be a little…impulsive, I guess you could say."

"Then shouldn't you have been watching him more closely?" Trey asked, scared and angry for his son's sake. "Why isn't he in school, where some teacher would at least be watching him?"

Reiger turned, startled, then eyed Trey with obvious suspicion. "Oh, we watch him, but he's a little hard to anticipate most of the time. We've had to get used to this sort of thing around here. The real trouble is that Jamie can be a bit clumsy at times and that doesn't go well with his impulses. Which is another reason not to climb up after him. I don't want to startle him. Excuse me," the vintner said and turned his attention back to the boy. "Did you hear me, James Gallagher Hopewell? I said come down," Reiger ordered again.

Trey couldn't help but wince at that name attached to his son. He'd never in a million years have given him his own, but neither would he have given him the name of the man who'd put an end to his marriage.

"Aw! I don't want to," Jamie shouted. "I just got up here."

"Now!" Reiger ordered.

Jamie began his descent, grumbling his disappointment with each step. Trey glanced at Will Reiger and noticed that the man at least seemed as nervous as he himself was. Then Jamie stepped onto a branch that snapped under his weight. And he tumbled.

Instinct alone made Trey rush beneath his son to catch him before he fell all the way to the ground. Jamie, rather than being appreciative, twisted and struggled, squealing as if he were in pain. Trey set him down as quickly as he could, but not before the boy had kicked him several times. The CD player in his jacket pocket fell out as Jamie's feet touched the ground. The boy wrenched away as if repulsed by Trey's touch. In a blink of an eye, he took off toward the winery. He ran as if the hounds of hell were nipping at his heels.

"I didn't mean to hurt him," Trey said as he picked up the expensive-looking CD player. He held it out to Reiger.

But the vintner stared at him for a long moment before nodding and taking the CD player. "Oh, I'm sure you didn't mean him any harm at all. Jamie often doesn't like to be touched. Are you here for a barrel tour or are you staying at Cliff Walk?"

"I checked in a while ago." Trey wiped the nervous sweat on his forehead. "I didn't expect my afternoon walk to be so eventful."

"No. I don't suppose you did. I expect I'll be seeing you around. Thank you for keeping the boy from hurting himself again," Reiger said and turned to go.

Again? The question arose in his mind. Was he talking about the incident in the drive or did he mean Jamie hurt himself often? Trey watched as Reiger followed along after Jamie toward the winery. What kind of people were raising his child? Apparently the kind who'd never thought to teach the boy any self-control, manners or discipline—but they bought him expensive toys?

Trey looked at his watch. Apparently they were also the kind of people who didn't always send a child to school on a school day.

Chapter Two

Caroline Hopewell checked the latest figures on the winery's new accounts, then absently pointed to her in-box. "Just stick the mail there, would you? I'll be done with this in a minute."

"Caro," her sister Abby said, her voice shaken.

Alarm shot through Caroline and put her every cell into overdrive even before she met her sister's worried gaze. Abby's creamy complexion was pale against her dark brown hair. "Is Jamie hurt?" She stood and sprinted around the desk and was halfway to the door before Abby answered.

"No. There's someone who wants to see you." Abby reached out and grabbed her hand. Caro couldn't help but notice her sister's fingers were icy-cold.

"Who on earth could have you this upset? Is it Harley Bryant?"

"No. It's someone staying at Cliff Walk. His reservation wasn't made in his name and then I didn't notice the name he signed when he registered. I'm sorry. I was busy and I hardly even looked at him. He stalked into the reception area just now looking for you. I'd already told him you were in before I turned around and actually got a look at him. That's when it all fell into place. I'm sure he's here about Jamie. You should have had more warning," Abby added, squeezing Caro's hand.

Caroline felt sick and confused as Abby sat on the settee in the corner of the office and pulled her down next to her. She hadn't even realized she'd moved. "Warning of what? *What* about this man fell into place? You aren't making sense."

"Who he is fell into place." Abby's deep brown eyes were anguished. "He looks exactly like Jamie. Or rather, *Jamie* looks like a young version of *him*."

She worked to process that and all its implications. "So Natalie had family after all. It must be a distant cousin or something. Relax. I have more of a claim than he would. I won't lose Jamie."

Abby shook her head, tears forming. "You don't have more than this guy. He's Natalie's ex-husband. It's Dr. Trey Westerly. I might never have liked or trusted Natalie, but even I never suspected she'd done this. She'd have plenty of explaining to do if she were still alive. To Father *and* Dr. Westerly. Now I'm afraid she's left you to deal with the fallout from her lies."

Was her brain misfiring? Why couldn't she grasp what Abby was saying? "Fallout? Lies?"

Abby's expression was a mix of pity and anxiety as she reached out and grasped her shoulder. The contact did nothing to ease her nerves. "He has to be Jamie's father, Caro."

Caroline could only stare. Numb and sick at once. Their father had been Jamie's father. And Jamie was *her* son now. True, he was really her half brother, but she'd adopted him in good faith and, more important to her way of thinking, Jamie had claimed her as his mother when he'd begun calling her "Mama" at two and a half and wouldn't be dissuaded. Over the past six years, through tougher times than most parents face, she and Jamie had bonded as mother and child.

Her heart started thundering. No one was going to waltz in from stage left and take her son away. No one! She forced herself to take a deep breath. "Let's not panic. Send him in and we'll see what questions he asks. And what questions he can answer for me. Putting off the inevitable is never a very productive way to tackle a problem."

"Yes, but he who runs away lives to fight another day," Abby muttered and faded back through the door. Caroline stood and returned to her desk, reaching for the picture of Jamie displayed prominently there. She found herself wondering what an adult version of her blond-haired, blue-eyed son would look like. Then the door pushed inward and she knew.

Trey Westerly was utterly devastating.

In every way.

Her heart pounding even faster than before, Caroline bounced to her feet, refusing to relinquish even a modicum of power to his overwhelming presence. "Dr. Westerly, I understand you wanted to speak to me. Please have a seat."

She stood waiting for the doctor to sit, all the while trying to still her pounding heart. It wouldn't do for him to know how much his presence unnerved her. He really was the image of Jamie—or rather, as Abby had pointed out, Jamie was the image of him.

Meanwhile, questions without answers swirled through Caro's thoughts. Did Dr. Westerly know the truth or not? And either way, what did he want? Had her father known the truth and claimed Jamie anyway?

She couldn't imagine James Hopewell voluntarily giving his name to another man's child, no matter how desperate he'd suddenly become to pass his name on. But that must be exactly what he'd done. Knowingly or not.

She also couldn't imagine this formidable man before her seeing Jamie and not putting two and two together. The subject of all her angst sat in the chair she'd indicated, but he didn't relax. He looked as tense as she felt. Tense and angry.

He knew. He had to know.

Still, she decided to pretend ignorance of the obvious facts. He'd come there under false pretenses, so she felt more than justified for any charade. "I hope everything at Cliff Walk is to your satisfaction," she said. "What can I do for you?"

"You can quit the act, for one thing. And for the record, not a thing has been to my satisfaction since my mother brought me this." He leaned forward to drop a newspaper clipping on the desk in front of her. Their fingers brushed as she automatically reached for it. They both yanked their hands back, allowing the clipping to fall to the desk.

Caroline shook her head in consternation. No one's touch had ever affected her like that. But then no one had ever been so great a threat to life as she knew it. She rubbed her fingers against her palm to banish the perplexing sensations, then she lifted the piece of newsprint to examine it. It was the article that had run in the Bucks County paper on the ribbon cutting. And a thought rose to haunt her: if she hadn't let Jamie attend, none of this would be happening.

"My mother recognized the boy as mine the moment she saw it," Dr. Westerly said.

Caroline carefully folded the paper and set it aside. She arranged her features in a noncommittal mask—a difficult task considering all that was at stake. But she wasn't about to give away anything of the panic and fear she felt at that moment. She cleared her throat of the thick emotion threatening to choke her. "Children often resemble adults who are no relation. I can't think you were all that sure of your claim or you'd have sent a lawyer instead of showing up on your own."

"I came here to get the lay of the land. To see how my son is faring here with you. I'm not heartless. I had no intention of disrupting the boy's world any more than necessary in order to become a part of his life. Now that I've seen him, however, I thank God I came here."

"Oh? And why is that?" she asked coolly.

"Are you aware that while you're in here running your family's little entrepreneurial enterprise, my son could have been killed climbing a tree that hangs over the side of a cliff? I caught him just in time to keep him from plummeting over twenty feet to the ground. If he'd been on the far side of the tree or if I hadn't been there—" He shook his head, clearly still upset over the memory.

Jamie often had that effect on the uninitiated. "Thank you," Caroline said, trying hard to be understanding even though she resented his very existence.

"Well, that's more than I got from him. He acted as if I'd squeezed the life out of him." Trey glared at her. "The child is out of control. Why on earth is he not in school at this hour?"

"He goes to a special school with unusual hours."

"Unusual?"

"He attends on a rolling schedule that allows me to accompany him one or two Saturdays a month. Other children have different days at the school with their parents." She didn't add that that day was more like a family counseling and learning day for parents. "Jamie has developmental problems."

"From where I'm sitting, it's you who has problems, Ms. Hopewell. Jamie is filthy. Undisciplined. He has no manners at all. And he seems intent on ending his life before he reaches age eight! Earlier, he ran in front of my car! I don't think he even realized he'd nearly been hit. He was wearing a Discman turned up so loud he didn't even hear the car. At the time he was running to catch up to your vintner, who as a babysitter is a complete failure!"

"How many other children do you and your wife have?" she asked, wondering if he'd found another woman who had overlooked his personality for his looks and money.

"I have no other children. One marriage was enough for me, thank you."

"Then what qualifies you to pass judgment on how I raise my son?"

"I was a kid myself once. I know what I know. And he's my son."

Striving too maintain her calm control but clinging to it by her fingernails, she said, "The state of Pennsylvania says otherwise. And I assure you you're over-reacting. Everything you've seen here today has a plausible explanation."

"I'd say you're *under*reacting." He raked a hand through his wheat-colored hair. "I need to see him. Talk to him."

Caro stared at Trey, panic beating an erratic pulse through her—all that she had built could be destroyed so easily. Jamie was doing better than his therapist had thought possible when he first had been diagnosed with Sensory Integration Dysfunction. Jamie's SID often caused people to pin labels on him like *undisciplined, aggressive* and a variety of other negative tags. Few strangers saw past his symptoms to the truth about her kindhearted and sensitive son.

As for her neglecting him, nothing could be further from the truth. Jamie had only come as far as he had because she'd been so aggressive about his therapy since the day his occupational therapist diagnosed him and set up a course of treatment. Between her, her family and a special school she herself had helped found for children with his and other similar problems, Jamie was doing remarkably well. He wasn't as yet a com-

KATE WELSH   37

pletely "normal" child, but he showed every promise of becoming one someday.

Caroline clenched her fists under the desk. She might understand Trey's reactions and his misreading of the situation, but that didn't mean she had to like it. Or put up with it. And it didn't give him the right to pass judgment on her parenting skills or on Jamie. She was sick and tired of people who didn't know all the facts discounting Jamie as a bad child.

And then there were all the things Natalie had told her about Dr. Trey Westerly. After getting to know Natalie, Caroline had come to the conclusion that her father's second wife had been a pawn in the hands of both her first and second husbands. Trey Westerly had ignored, belittled and cheated on Natalie until she'd contemplated suicide. Instead she'd confided her anguish to the man who had taken her on as an intern, filling her lonely life with purpose. James Hopewell had been only too happy to console the lonely, broken young woman. Then he'd given her even more purpose in life. He'd given her Jamie.

But, of course, now it appeared he hadn't even given her a child to care about at all. Caroline didn't think her father had had any intention of ending his marriage of twenty-three years in order to marry Natalie. It hadn't escaped Caro's notice that their father had only come clean about the affair and asked for a divorce after Natalie's ultrasound confirmed that the child she carried was a boy. And by then Natalie's husband had already discarded her.

Love. That was the culprit. Romantic love turned

people into manipulative, deceitful copies of their former selves. It caused them to build up unrealistic expectations for their partners in the insanity of being in love. Then, when those impossible hopes and dreams fell through and love died, the mere humans left to deal with the fallout had few options that didn't include hurting someone.

Romance was to blame for all of it, but that didn't exonerate Trey Westerly in Caroline's eyes.

She stood and squared her shoulders. Her knees quaked, but Trey Westerly didn't have to know that. Jamie had come too far to subject him to the man who'd single-handedly almost driven his biological mother to attempt suicide. When Caroline adopted Jamie, she'd embraced the many aspects of motherhood, and one of those was as Jamie's protector.

"Dr. Westerly, as I've said, you have no right to come in here and comment on a situation you know nothing about. Jamie is my son. I've raised him since he was a colicky, fussy eight-month-old who no one wanted. Notices were placed in any number of newspapers, looking for a relative—New York City's included. No one—least of all you—came forward, so I adopted him. The adoption was meticulously legal.

"Now, after years have passed, you suddenly storm in here making wild claims and nasty comments. You came here unannounced, under an assumed name to spy on us. As for you meeting Jamie, that isn't going to happen. You have no right or claim to him. I won't have him unsettled that way."

"You can't keep my child from me. DNA testing will show I'm his father."

His threat stunned her, but she summoned the courage to face him down for Jamie's sake. "It might. *If* I allowed such testing. I can assure you I won't." She crossed her arms. "Now, before I have to call the police, I suggest you vacate your room at Cliff Walk and get off Hopewell property. You aren't welcome here."

Dr. Westerly stood and raised an eyebrow. He looked cool and confident, which was the direct opposite of how Caro felt. "I suppose that means you'll be hearing from my lawyer after all, Ms. Hopewell."

"How come I had to have that test?" Jamie demanded, worrying at his cheek as if trying to erase the feel of the cotton swab. "I hated it. A lot!"

She'd fought that test and held it up for as long as she'd been able. It had been two weeks since the court order had come down, and after that she'd even dared to delay complying as long as possible without risking contempt charges. It was now a month since Wesley Westerly III had appeared and turned her life upside down.

Only years of learning to think before giving away her feelings with a careless gesture kept Caroline from releasing an audible sigh at Jamie's question. They had been over this so many times already. She'd known going in how much having that seemingly insignificant test would bother Jamie. She'd been right. She also knew that only a very small majority of children would have even thought twice about having their cheek swabbed. But Jamie was firmly back in his sensory-avoidance mode, and with that came hypersensitivity to touch and sound. He'd been back to his normal self—

or what passed for normal with Jamie—since the afternoon he'd climbed the tree. His fall seemed to have triggered the change.

A rarity for Jamie, he'd been in a sensory-seeking period that week until the fall. That explained his sudden need to touch everything that came into his sphere. It had caused his headlong rush up the tree and his rapture at the feel of the wind on his skin. And of course it was the reason his headphones had been turned up so high that he hadn't heard Trey Westerly's car. Jamie had been subconsciously seeking the sensory input of the loud music. It was during these infrequent periods that Jamie was often injured.

Since his fall into Trey's arms—or maybe because of it—Jamie had returned to his usual sensory-avoiding mode of behavior. He kept his headphones turned on softly—more as a buffer from the world than to experience sound. He couldn't stand to wear any restrictive clothing, and getting dirty frightened him. The very texture of soil or sand offended his heightened sensitivity to touch. He also shied from it because getting dirty meant washing the dirt off later, which necessitated the feel of a washcloth on his body. Even his eating habits were different right now.

A picky eater at best, Jamie couldn't handle certain textures of food either. Oatmeal made from cut oats was fine, but he hated the kind made from rolled oats. He'd turned against mashed potatoes last week because there'd been a few lumps in them.

Reasons notwithstanding, the bottom line was the test had been a traumatic event to Jamie and he couldn't put it out of his head. In fact, he'd fixated on it. His therapist suggested Caroline commiserate with his feelings, then try to distract him from his fixation on what he saw as an invasion of his space.

Just that morning Caroline had taken him to see his psychologist. She had suggested that if the fixation lasted this long, the test needed to be explained and the blame focused on something nebulous like the court order Caroline hadn't dare defy. She was not to bring his father's name or his request for the test into the explanation lest it cause later problems. Caroline had known that already, of course. The hope was that once Jamie had an entity to blame for the outrage, he would be able to move on.

Now Caroline recognized that it was indeed time to get this behind them. She took a slow, fortifying breath as she ran the soft baby hairbrush over Jamie's legs. She tried humming along with the therapeutic CD that played in the background, reaching for calm herself. "I know the test bothered you, angel, and I'm sorry for that. You had to have the test because a judge at family court said you had to. But it's all over now and we can forget it."

The trouble was that now that the results were in, forgetting them wasn't an option. She'd also gotten advice on how to explain the sudden appearance of Trey, but even with expert advice, it still filled her heart with dread.

Her lawyer had warned her weeks ago that they were going to wind up in court again. Trey Westerly had filed papers that afternoon almost moments after the positive DNA test results had been delivered.

Jamie tried to shy away from the brush, but she kept

on with the strange-looking but effective therapy. And she forged ahead with an even more onerous task. "Jamie, you remember about your adoption, don't you?" she said as nonchalantly as possible.

Uncertainty entered Jamie's eyes as soon as she mentioned his adoption. "You aren't going to give me back, are you? I don't mean to be a bad boy, Mama."

Caroline's heart shattered. "You are not bad! We've talked about that. Look at all the things you can do that you didn't used to be able to do. You are my son. Now and always. That's what the adoption said and I wouldn't give you up for anything. But it turns out that I'm not your sister the way we all thought."

Jamie frowned and turned over, staring at her wide-eyed. "How come?"

"My father wasn't your father after all. And that's really good news. Do you know why?"

Jamie's frown stayed in place in spite of the upbeat tone she'd used. He shook his head, looking more unsure by the moment.

"Because it turns out that you have a real, live dad. He was married to your birth mother, Natalie, before she married James, my father. She must not have known you were on the way when she got divorced from your father and married mine."

"Divorce is like what happened to Tommy Daily's mom and dad. And then his mom got married and he has two dads now."

Caro nodded. "Exactly. And you've met your dad already. He saved you when you fell out of the tree."

Jamie's expression turned instantly mutinous. "I don't like him. He hurt me. Do I have to see him again?"

"I'm sure he never meant to hurt you. He saved you when he caught you. I know falling and finding a stranger holding you was upsetting, but he was only trying to help. And I'm glad he did or you might have been hurt. As far as you seeing him, I can't answer that right now. This is all pretty new information and I don't know what the court will say about you seeing him."

Caro realized her mistake the second the word left her mouth, and Jamie confirmed her worst fear an instant later. "Court?" he demanded. "Is he why I had to have that test? Did he make me have the test?" Once again he rubbed the inside of his cheek with his tongue.

"The test was the only way the court could be sure he was your dad. It was the court who gave the order."

"I don't want a dad. I have you. And Aunt Sam and Aunt Abby. Grandmom and Uncle Will. He had a mean face. I didn't like him."

Though Caroline was heartened by Jamie's loyalty, she also knew she had to find a way to help him come to terms with the changes that were bound to come into his life. Trey Westerly existed, and even if she managed to keep him out of Jamie's life, Jamie wouldn't be a child forever.

Chapter Three

Caroline still hadn't come up with a way to help Jamie adjust when family court convened the next Friday. She was still stunned at the speed with which the court had scheduled the custody hearing, but AJ Cunningham, the family's attorney, assured her that their side was more than ready. Her heart pounded as she walked into the informal courtroom.

Caroline looked around. The rich, dark wainscoting that was so reminiscent of Hopewell Manor did nothing to make her feel at ease. Nor did the red-and-navy Persian carpet that was a near twin to the one in Cliff Walk's day room. Accompanied by her family and Will Reiger, she walked toward the wide conference table. Putting her hand out to AJ Cunningham, Caroline greeted the lawyer who had seen them through the dif-

ficult days following her father's death and through all
its financial implications. He took her hand, but Caro's
attention was drawn partly to Trey, though she tried
without success to ignore his overwhelming presence.

Sitting on the other side of the big conference table,
Dr. Wesley Westerly III dominated the room and her
thoughts even with his back to her. She swore she could
smell him across the room.

A shiver traced her spine as she asked AJ, "Did you
get Jamie's therapists listed as witnesses in time?"

The kindly lawyer smiled. "Every last one. Don't
you worry. Judge Feingold is fair. *And* she's a mother.
I told you she's not going to wrench Jamie away from
you. Westerly, in his zeal to get this before the court,
got himself the best judge for our side."

"But you admitted she has the power to take Jamie
away," Caroline said as the bailiff called the court into
session and the judge walked in with her black robes
flowing, her gray hair curling around her lined face.
Caro stared at the woman who would decide her fate
and her son's as she automatically stood, then sat down
at the appropriate time next to AJ. Her mother and sisters filed into the chairs behind her.

While the judge shuffled some papers, Caro glanced
across the table and noticed an older woman lean forward to talk to Trey. Her eyes strayed and pinned Caroline with a venomous glare. If looks really could kill,
Caro thought, Jamie would be a resident of New York
by bedtime because she would have been well on her
way to her grave.

After all the witnesses were called, the judge studied them both for a long moment before speaking.

"Well, now. We've all heard extensive medical and psychological profiles with opposing views. I commend Ms. Hopewell for her aggressive approach to her son's problems and must say in deference to Dr. Westerly's expert witness, Jamie's progress is irrefutable. Life with Jamie has not been easy, has it?" she asked Caro.

"I love my son, Your Honor," she stated. "I don't find anything a chore if it helps him."

The judge nodded kindly. "That's good to hear. I find the claims the plaintiff has made disturbing, especially as they are inconsistent with the testimony of Jamie's teachers and therapists. Caroline Hopewell is, as far as the state and this court is concerned, a good mother." Her eyes sharpened as she glanced across the table. "And she *is* his mother, make no mistake about that. I studied Jamie's adoption papers and everything is in impeccable order. All the i's are dotted and the t's crossed."

Caroline shot Trey a smug grin, but then Judge Feingold said the one word no one wanted to hear in a proceeding like this, and it made Caro's heart stutter.

"However...I must take the father's rights into account, too. Judson versus Coldwater clearly..."

Trey looked away from Caroline Hopewell's sudden look of horror and tried to listen intently to what the judge was saying. But her words floated away, because Caroline's fear of losing Jamie was nearly a palpable entity in the room. Her wavy blond hair and green eyes drew his attention easily enough, but her fear sucked him in like the eddy of an undertow. He couldn't help but feel guilty for turning her world upside down like this.

And he was also distracted by the testimony her experts had given. He'd discounted what Caroline's witnesses had said, listening with only half an ear and stubbornly believing the man recommended to him by a colleague at the hospital. His expert had diagnosed Jamie with Attention-Deficit/Hyperactivity Disorder. He'd said it was a disgrace that a child with ADHD wasn't on a drug to help him calm down enough to function. He'd called Jamie's SID diagnosis "voodoo science."

Now Trey was sorry he hadn't listened to the opposing viewpoints. His thoughts stuttered to a stop. Maybe he hadn't because that might mean he had to look at his own early life too closely. He shook off the thought. Whatever had stopped him, whatever was wrong with Jamie, Trey wouldn't walk away from his child, as he often felt his father had done to him in his younger years.

"...so while I will not overturn the adoption," the judge was saying, "I do feel Dr. Westerly would be an asset in Jamie's life. So after careful consideration, I think we need to treat this somewhat like a divorce situation. I am prepared to grant Dr. Westerly limited visitation rights, with all custodial rights remaining with the boy's mother."

"But Your Honor, Jamie can't just be expected to go visit a complete stranger," Caroline interjected. In spite of AJ Cunningham's hand on her arm, tightening the more she said, she went on. "You said you'd read his file. Jamie isn't going to handle this as easily as another child might."

Rather than react negatively to Caroline's outburst,

the judge smiled gently. "Indeed, I have read his file. And I understood his therapist and I sympathize with your concern. Dr. Westerly, you need to get to know your son and the environment he's used to. Normal children get dirty. They climb trees and do things that are dangerous. My son, of whom I am quite proud, ate worms on a dare at Jamie's age. He upchucked them in the midst of the guests at the first judicial dinner party I hosted." The judge's smile grew, a fond memory crinkling her dark eyes. "He's a well-respected rabbi today."

Her gaze sharpened then and she pinned him with a commanding look. "Dr. Westerly, it is you who must find a way to acclimate Jamie into your world so that visits to your home won't be frightening to him. Considering that you reside in New York City, that won't be easy. You also need to learn all you can about your son's specific needs. It wouldn't do to undermine the progress his mother and his therapists have made. I'm prepared to allow the families to work out how to best accomplish all of that. We will recess for half an hour to work out something that the court can agree with. After hearing what you come up with, I will revisit the case in three months. At which time we'll work out a permanent arrangement."

With that pronouncement Judge Feingold stood and floated through a door to the left of her chair, leaving stunned silence in her wake.

"Well, now," Cunningham said, breaking the stalemate of stares from both sides of the table. "How do you propose to get to know the boy, Westerly?"

Trey felt his pulse thunder. Him? It was on him? He

knew nothing at all about children unless they were his patients. "I guess I could stay at Cliff Walk for a couple weekends, then take him home with me for a week or two."

"Absolutely not," Caroline all but shouted. "I will not have you thrusting yourself into his life and frightening Jamie by taking him away to a strange place after only a brief acquaintance. Especially since he doesn't like you even a little bit."

Trey was unaccountably hurt. "I didn't do a thing to earn his dislike. I caught him when he fell! That's all the contact I've had with him. What have you told him?"

"Nothing but that you exist and who you are."

"Then how can the child dislike his father?" Charles Davenport, Trey's lawyer, probed. "What have you been saying to him about Dr. Westerly?"

Her lawyer cleared his throat. "If you are implying Caroline is trying to poison the well, let me assure you she would never malign Dr. Westerly because he is the boy's father, and that would hurt Jamie. The problem is that the boy holds you responsible for the DNA test he had to endure."

Endure? It was a cotton swab, for heaven's sake! Trey thought, then sucked in a shocked breath. A memory from his childhood surfaced in a blinding flash. He'd had a bad sore throat and the doctor had taken a culture of his throat. The feel of that cotton had sent him into the temper tantrum that had landed him in boarding school.

"And who told him the test was my client's fault?" Davenport demanded before Trey could completely bring himself out of his distressing thoughts. He winced. Charles was a topflight family lawyer, but that didn't make his abrasive personality any easier to take.

"The judge isn't going to take kindly to your having poisoned my grandson's mind against his father. Charles, make a note to bring that up when Her Honor returns," Mrs. Westerly interjected.

Caroline's green eyes widened with outrage and she gripped the table, her fingertips going white from the pressure. Before Trey could say anything to defuse the building confrontation, she spat out her reply. "I did no such thing! That test disturbed him terribly. It has preyed on his mind. I only did what his psychologist advised. I told him the court had ordered the test so he'd have someone to pin the blame on. We hoped then he could let go of the memory and move on. Jamie is a bright little boy, though, and he put it all together with learning Dr. Westerly exists and that the court would decide if he'd have to see him again. I tried to tell Jamie having a father was a good thing, but he isn't interested. He's happy the way things are. Why couldn't you have just left us alone?" she demanded, her voice cracking with emotion as her anguished gaze bored into his.

Trey felt another pang of guilt, but that emotion was quickly overshadowed with anger. Why couldn't she see *his* side? He pushed away from the table and walked across the room. But getting away from her didn't help. He wouldn't desert his son! He whirled and fired back his answer to her outrageous question. "I couldn't leave you alone, because my ex-wife and your father stole my son! A son I never knew about. And I have a right to know him. He has a right to know me!"

She slapped the table. "He doesn't *want* to know you. And what about Jamie's right to be secure? What about his right to the only life he knows?"

Charles started tossing papers in his briefcase. "This is a waste of time, Trey. We'll take this to New York's family court. I told you before we filed here that as a respected New York resident you could expect a much more favorable ruling there. Maybe even see the adoption overturned."

Trey didn't want that, but when the Hopewell lawyer confirmed that it was possible New York would side with him, Juliana, Caroline's mother, spoke up. "Caro," she said quietly, "in the long run it would be in Jamie's best interest to get to know his father, as the judge suggested." Caroline looked as shocked as if her mother had slapped her.

Trey's mother laid her hand on his arm. "I think you should listen to Charles, Trey. Those women aren't even blood relatives to the boy. He'll adjust to living with you, and Abraham Bishop Academy will take care of all these supposed problems. Children are resilient and trainable."

Trey felt a lump form in his stomach that reminded him of the way he'd felt when his mother had taken him to the Academy and left him there. He couldn't keep evading the truth. Jamie wasn't so different from the way he'd been. More pronounced in all instances, but the things he'd heard since the hearing began reminded him of feelings and urges he'd learned to keep prisoner of an iron control before they'd eased then finally disappeared. He'd done it for years in trade for the privilege of living in his mother's home. Of being his mother's son.

Had he somehow passed on this SID to his son? Were Jamie's difficulties his fault? His mother was apparently wrong about a lot of things to do with raising children. Especially about Jamie. He glanced at Caroline and saw her fearful, tortured expression. Something he'd thought about that first day came back to him in that moment of clarity. There were other victims in this mess besides him.

Jamie had had everything he knew about his life proven false. James Hopewell wasn't his father. Samantha and Abigail weren't his sisters and neither was Caroline. He no longer had a part in the not-inconsiderable Hopewell heritage.

And Caroline? She must have changed her entire young life for Jamie. At twenty-two she'd taken on the responsibility for a baby rather than let the state find him a family. Now Trey had walked in and questioned her motives and methods and threatened to take away the person she'd built her life around. If she hadn't done that, he'd never have found his son at all. Which meant he owed her something other than fear and loss.

He tried to block out the rest of the people in the room and focused only on her—the woman his son loved as a mother. It was frighteningly easy. He stared at her, willing her to look him in the eye. When she glanced his way again, he felt the sharp edge of some dark emotion stab his gut. Her green eyes darkened as their gazes locked, held. After a few disturbing moments she blinked and gave her head a small but vigorous shake. But like him, ignoring the others was no great task. Like him, she was unable to look away.

"I'm perfectly willing to let the adoption stand with

a fair visitation agreement," he told her, still holding her gaze, still captive of hers. "But I need help getting to know Jamie."

"I think Dr. Westerly is right," Juliana Hopewell said, finally freeing them. Both were able to look away from each other then, and he breathed a grateful sigh of relief.

"Wesley, don't be foolish. They have only their interests in mind," his mother whispered.

He ignored her. "What do you have in mind Mrs. Hopewell?" he asked Juliana.

"I think you should spend two or three *weeks*—not days—at Cliff Walk getting to know your son. Then, during the rest of the allotted time before the judge examines this again, Caroline should supervise weekend visits to your home. Jamie will need her with him in the unfamiliar surroundings. One weekend should probably be spent in New York and the next at the winery. During those Pennsylvania visits, Jamie should stay at the B and B with you to get him used to being alone with you while he's in a setting he finds comfortable."

"I'm perfectly able to help Trey acclimate the boy to life in New York," Trey heard his mother say. "We can take trips to the museums. Go shopping. Get out and about in the hustle and bustle of the city."

Trey remembered his first terrifying trip to Manhattan. Before he could point out the obvious—that Jamie would hate it and that she was as much a stranger to the boy as he was—Samantha Hopewell, Caro's sister, did the deed for him. "Mrs. Guilford, you don't know squat about this kid if you think you can do that with him and not be sorry you tried," she snapped.

"Well! It hardly seems fair to give her access to Jamie on Trey's weekends," his mother retorted to their lawyer.

"It will if Jamie goes ballistic in the middle of New York City," the youngest sister, Abigail, said quietly, laying a restraining hand on her sister Samantha's arm. "Or if he gets so agitated he runs out into traffic. That could just as easily happen."

Meanwhile, Caroline's gaze had ping-ponged from person to person as they each spoke, her anxiety clearly rising as the tone of the room began to heat again. Even Abby's calm tone did nothing to change the look of abject panic on her beautiful face.

At the cost of annoying his mother, Trey broke in, needing to do something for the woman who'd taken such dedicated care of his son. "This isn't about me, Mother. This is about making Jamie comfortable and minimizing the impact on his emotions that my entrance into his life has apparently caused. What do you say, Ms. Hopewell? Shall we give it a try your mother's way? Can we work this out together for Jamie's sake?"

Juliana stood and put her hand on her daughter's shoulder. When Caroline looked over her shoulder, her mother nodded as if reassuring Caroline that it would all work out.

"All right," Caroline said after a few deep breaths that made her small breasts rise and fall invitingly.

Trey looked away, embarrassed that he should even notice something like that at a time like this. Finally, his errant thoughts once more under control, he looked back at her a moment later. This time, however, he studiously kept his gaze directed above her shoulders. She was obviously deep in thought, a small crease pleating the skin between her gently arched eyebrows.

"Call and let us know when you'll arrive so we can reserve a room for you. We can work out the rest of the arrangements when you get to Cliff Walk. I'll talk to Jamie's therapists and find the best way to let him know what will be happening. Just understand that none of this will be easy."

It took Trey the entire weekend and every favor owed to him, but he'd lined up replacement surgeons to cover for him at the hospital. Ruefully he realized there were some advantages to being tied to an E.R. and the vagaries of accidents and crimes. Emergencies might constantly interrupt his downtime, but when he managed to line up cover, he was free as a bird with no set schedule promised to regular patients.

He'd called Cliff Walk yesterday to alert Caroline of his imminent arrival but hadn't spoken to her. Her sister, Abigail, had been cool and formal, promising to relay his message. And to say his mother wasn't on board with his capitulation in court was an understatement. His lawyer, Charles Davenport, wasn't happy either with what he saw as a blotch on his nearly perfect record. But to Trey, Jamie's happiness was the most important thing, and if Caroline Hopewell was vital to that happiness then the hearing Davenport had pushed for in New York family court would never happen.

As he tooled along the twisting road next to the river and the canal, Trey glanced into the backseat at the set of rackets and bucket of balls he'd brought along. He could hardly restrain the excitement that had been building since that morning when he'd noticed the tennis courts advertised in Cliff Walk's brochure. He'd realized he could play tennis with his son. He hoped that maybe teaching Jamie the game the way his father had taught him would open a door between the two of them.

When Trey thought back to those days before his parents' divorce, he felt a surge of nostalgia. His father used to take him down to the courts and play for hours amidst laughter and camaraderie. His heart constricted painfully. Everything had changed with the divorce—including where he lived most of the year—but no one could take away those early memories. And now he was going to begin building good memories with his son.

He'd called Hopewell again to ask if Jamie played tennis and he'd gotten Abigail on the phone that time, too. At first she'd clearly been surprised at his question. She'd said no. Jamie had nearly no sports equipment and didn't seem inclined toward athletics. It had been a halting admission. Trey imagined she was afraid he'd somehow use the knowledge against Caroline. He could only hope time and his attitude would take care of the mistrust his suit had caused.

Now, because he'd stopped to buy tennis gear, he was running late. But it would be worth it just to see Jamie's reaction to the gift. But first he had to formally meet his son. He hoped it went better than their first encounter at the tree.

The bed-and-breakfast looked every bit as welcoming as it had the last time, but Abigail Hopewell's dark eyes were now shadowed with worry. "I put you in the same room you were in before," she said as she rounded the tall desk at the back of the foyer and handed him his room key. "Caroline and Jamie are in the back parlor. Jamie's been terrified since she had to tell him about you coming here."

Trey tried to explain. "Look, Ms. Hopewell, I didn't create this situation. My ex-wife did. Natalie's the one who made sure I was kept out of Jamie's life—not me."

She raised one dark eyebrow and tossed her head, sending her dark, wavy hair floating over her shoulders. She sighed. "I was only trying to soften the blow if he rejects you. And as for Natalie, I was always leery of what was going on in her head. Any idea how she rationalized this mess she created?"

He'd wondered but he'd conceded that it would take a trip inside Natalie's seriously distorted mind to find an answer. And the answer probably wouldn't make sense anyway. He was nearly certain Nat had been unbalanced. He should have seen it before marrying her, or at least rather than drift from one argument to the next, he should have seen that she got help. But he'd been too involved in medical school and hadn't taken the time to force the issue.

"I can't imagine. But *she* probably did—imagine a reason, I mean. Nat was like that. Half her realities were realities to only herself. But I can't think about it anymore. Now is all I care about. I'd like to see Jamie." He pointed past the desk down a hall next to the winding staircase. "This way?"

"Last door on the right. I wouldn't expect too much too soon from either of them." Without another word Abigail pivoted away and walked into the formal dining room on the other side of the foyer. Continuing through the beautifully appointed Victorian room, she pushed through a swinging door, leaving him alone to listen to his own troubled thoughts and the ticktock of a seven-foot-tall grandfather clock.

Trey stared after her. So was Abigail on his side? He hoped so or he'd need to sleep with one eye open for the next three weeks, he thought wryly. Like her blond oldest sister, Abigail had a protective streak a mile wide where Jamie was concerned, and that was a good thing. It was, after all, his son they all cared about. But still, he wondered not for the first time what Nat had said about him that had sparked such instant wariness in all the Hopewells.

He sighed and ran a hand through his hair. God only knew. By the time Jamie must have been conceived, he and Natalie fought more than they did anything else. And about more trumped-up crazy charges than he could recount. He'd long since questioned her sanity and had begun to doubt his own.

It was a small miracle Jamie existed at all. But he had reconstructed the events that led to his son's conception. Trey had come home from the hospital exhausted after spending nearly forty-eight hours awake and on his feet. And Nat had been there crying and spouting insane accusations of mental cruelty and unfaithfulness. It wasn't the first time. This time, though, he'd decided that since arguing would take more time and energy than he'd had, he would just try to prove to her that she was the only woman he wanted. She'd been gone when he'd woken sometime late the next day. He'd figured his lovemaking had failed to show her what she needed. When he was served with divorce papers a week later, he'd been almost relieved.

Apparently, though, he hadn't failed to give her a baby. He hadn't suspected anything was amiss because as far as he'd known she was on the pill. When she'd filed the divorce papers, he'd tried not to feel like a failure and counted himself lucky and well out of a disastrous marriage. Now he wondered if Nat hadn't used him like a stud to trap James Hopewell into divorcing his wife and marrying her.

Had Jamie been nothing more than her ticket to greener pastures?

Jamie's squeal of delight and Caroline's gentle laughter floated up the hall toward him, and Trey's dark thoughts evaporated. It also set him in motion. The past was past. Down that hall lay his future.

Chapter Four

"You two look as if you're having a good time. Mind if I join you?"

Caroline looked up at the sound of Trey Westerly's voice. He stood in the doorway looking cosmopolitan and annoyingly handsome. As she sat up and turned to face Jamie's father, the clock in the foyer struck two. Trey Westerly was a full hour late. He'd probably spent the whole time in front of a mirror making sure he looked perfect.

Because of Natalie's tales of her marriage, Caro had suspected he'd be late, but she'd hesitated to say anything to Jamie. She'd been warned by his therapist that she'd have to walk a fine line between not speaking ill of her son's father and readying him for a relationship that might not be all a little boy could hope for in his

heart of hearts. Guilt sliced through her and she acknowledged that she'd failed Jamie in this instance.
She should have found some way to prepare Jamie for
his father's carelessness and neglect. She consoled herself that Trey's conduct wasn't yet a problem, but still,
the upsetting anticipation of this dreaded meeting had
been drawn out.

Instead of addressing the difficult subject, she'd
coaxed Jamie into lying on the floor so she could read
him his favorite book to distract him from thoughts of
his meeting with Trey. Time had slipped away and
though she'd thought she'd kept Jamie calm, when she
felt him stiffen next to her she realized he'd been tense
all along.

"Dr. Westerly, I see you've finally arrived," Caro
said with fake cheer.

He seemed to know she was annoyed, though she
would have sworn she'd hidden her feelings. She had
to learn to be more circumspect. "I'm sorry I'm late. I
stopped off to pick up something for Jamie and got a
little overwhelmed in the store. Maybe a little later you
and I can take a look at what I bought. What do you say,
Jamie?"

Jamie frowned. "I say lots of stuff but I can't talk to
you. You're a stranger." He crossed his thin arms and
scowled stubbornly.

"Jamie," Caro said, reaching for patience. He was
more resistant to meeting Trey than she'd anticipated,
and she'd talked herself blue—apparently to no avail.
"We discussed this. Dr. Westerly is your father. He isn't
a stranger." She paused and thought better of her flat
statement. What if he tried to take Jamie? More cau-

tiously she added, "You don't know him yet, but I told you it is okay to talk to him. No one is expecting you to go off with him. He just wants to get to know you."

Caro watched Jamie look up at Trey, his golden-blond bowl-cut hair nearly covering his eyes. They were going to have to tackle a haircut again soon. It was a chore Jamie hated. He always reacted as if he could feel each hair being painfully severed.

She imagined Jamie was nothing like the son Trey thought he'd find when he'd come there. She'd sat in court in stunned horror as the independent educator his lawyer had insisted on calling in made his report. He'd said Jamie was average in height and weight. Bright. Accident-prone, easily upset and overstimulated. He'd labeled him with ADHD. He'd never talked to Jamie or his teacher but had stood behind the one-way-mirrored observation window in Jamie's classroom. He'd watched, reporting each problem and advising stricter discipline and drugs for Jamie, not therapy.

He'd slanted his testimony to sound as if Jamie's problems were the fault of his environment. In other words, her fault. Holly Oak Academy's fault. Luckily the judge had dismissed the charge out of hand, listening instead to the evaluation of the professionals who'd been involved for four years in Jamie's therapy.

She'd been angry and almost willing to let Trey try understanding Jamie on his own. But worry for her son's welfare would never have let that happen. Then there had come that long, magnetic moment between her and Trey at the hearing. She'd known then that she had to find a way to work with him for Jamie's sake—and for some unknown reason, for Trey's sake, too.

"Actually I wondered if you'd like to come along while Jamie and I get that gift I mentioned out of the car?" Trey invited when Jamie continued to stare at him in silence.

Caro looked at her watch. She had piles of work to do, but Jamie was frozen in place and Trey Westerly didn't look any more comfortable than her son. She had to help ease Jamie into this relationship whether she wanted to or not. Whether she thought she could handle being near Trey or not.

She told herself she had to check out the gift anyway to make sure it was appropriate for Jamie. "I can't wait to see your present, Jamie. Aren't you excited?"

When Jamie remained stubbornly silent, Trey asked, "Don't you want to see what I brought you, son?"

His curiosity got the better of him then. Jamie bounced up off the floor, tripped over absolutely nothing and cannoned into Trey. Jamie scrunched his shoulders as Trey caught him and righted him. It was easy to see how much Trey hated to let go, but he did.

Jamie stared down at Trey's feet. "Sorry I messed up your sneakers."

Trey looked down at the smudge Jamie's small feet had left in their wake. "I imagine they're washable," he said, his tone stiff, as if he'd never seen dirty sneakers before.

"Around here we just let the dirt fall where it will," Caro told him, trying to lighten the moment. "This is essentially a farm. A glorified one to be sure, but if we washed our shoes for every smudge, they'd wear out in the washing machine instead of on our feet."

Trey looked down at Jamie's feet. "I guess they would," he said, a frown wrinkling his forehead.

What was wrong with the man? If he didn't unbend a little, his stiffness would put Jamie off more than his very existence already had. "Let's go see your present, Jamie," she suggested and took his hand. "Lead on, Doctor."

"Call me Trey. We probably shouldn't be so formal."

Jamie frowned deeply, staring at his father. "How come your mama named you something so dumb?" he asked as they entered the foyer.

"It's just a nickname, sport. Because I'm the third person in a row in our family with my name. That's what Trey means. I was named for my father and grandfather."

"Me, too," Jamie said and Trey stiffened, but more importantly so did Jamie. Then he scowled again. "But not anymore because you're my real dad. So I'm just named after Mama's dad. Now that I have a different dad, do I have to get a new name, too, Mama? He called me *Sport*. Is *Sport* gonna be my name now? I don't like it. I liked being Jamie."

She smiled gently down at him. One never knew what children would get into their heads, especially hers. Not for the first time she wished kids came with instructions written on their heels. "You're still Jamie, honey. Trey called you sport as sort of another nickname. It's called a 'term of endearment.' It means he likes you. As he told you, Trey is a nickname, too. Your father's whole name is Dr. Wesley Westerly III."

Jamie looked horrified. "I'm glad my first mama didn't know he was my father. I much rather be James Gallagher Hopewell." Jamie looked up at Trey and smirked. She could see the zinger headed their way, but she also knew she couldn't do this for them completely. She wanted Trey to field this one himself. "You have a really dumb name," Jamie said.

Trey winced. "Trey doesn't sound so bad now, does it?" he muttered and walked through the front door toward his car.

Jamie went to follow, but Caro held on to his hand, keeping him in place. "Jamie, we spoke about showing respect to adults."

"Sorry, but his name is really dumb, Mama." He was none too quiet about his objection.

Thankfully Trey chuckled, albeit a little stiffly. "It is," he said as he turned toward them from the bottom of the steps. "And for the record, you wouldn't have been named Wesley even if I'd known you were my son when you were born. The first time I got beat up at school over my name I promised not to do that to any child of mine. Jamie is just fine."

"You have a father?" Jamie asked, his face screwed up in confusion.

Trey grinned, thinking of his kind, laid-back father as he opened the car door to pull out a bucket of brightly colored balls and two tennis rackets. "I have a terrific father. And while he was an utter failure at picking out names for little boys, he was great at teaching them things. I was right around your age when he taught me to play tennis. I thought since there are courts here, I could teach you. Sort of continue the tradition."

Jamie stared down at the bucket of balls with a mixture of fear and fatalism. Then he looked at her and she saw his disappointment as he clutched her hand tighter. He'd wanted Trey to instinctively know his limitations.

Jamie wasn't able to catch a ball because he couldn't seem to process how fast the ball was coming at him and therefore when to close his hand around it. It was the reason he didn't like sports of any kind.

But a tennis racket had a big area to hit with and not close to the body, so maybe he'd find he could handle it. "Let's go try it, Jamie," she encouraged. "It might be fun."

But Jamie couldn't hit the ball even when Trey slowly tossed it right at the racket. He swung too late and the ball just dropped to the ground or at best rolled away. So Trey tried to have Jamie throw the balls to him, which would have worked but when Trey returned the ball and it came flying back at him, Jamie shrieked and covered his head. And he kept on screaming even after Trey dropped his racket and tried to comfort him.

After only half an hour in his father's company it was obvious Jamie was more than ready to go home. And Caroline was more than ready to take him. It had been difficult being seated across a desk from Trey and later across a table in a confrontational court appearance. But watching him try and fail to win Jamie over or to even understand why he'd failed was exhausting. Her reactions to the man just made no sense.

She wasn't stupid or without experience. She'd finally understood what he made her feel even if she didn't understand why. She was attracted to him. *Blindly* attracted, it seemed, considering what his mere existence had done to her life and her son's.

Caro couldn't even point to one particular trait that

attracted her. Trey was certainly handsome, but she met and dealt with a lot of handsome men in the wine business. And he was apparently successful, but then again, so were most of the winery's wholesale customers who she'd dealt with over the years. Romantically speaking, Caroline hadn't given a man a second's thought since her father's infidelity to her mother and Kyle Winston's defection. All she knew was she could still remember Trey's scent long after she'd taken Jamie a mile away to Hopewell Manor. It was as if he'd become embedded in her brain.

When she was young and foolish, she'd come up with a bunch of general traits and put them on an imaginary list of pros and cons. That list had spelled out her ideal man. What was really annoying was that Trey Westerly would have more items on the con side of that imaginary list than any man she'd ever met—her former disloyal fiancé included—and yet she was *still* attracted to him.

It made no sense. He was stiff and overly formal with Jamie even when she could tell he was trying not to be. He'd apparently been unfaithful to Natalie, which gave him a big strike in the loyalty category. He seemed nearly compulsive about cleanliness. She'd seen that herself in the way he'd talked about Jamie that first day and his reaction to the condition of Jamie's shoes. After their first meeting it was clear he was critical, too. And he seemed to keep himself in iron control at all times, which gave credence to Natalie's claims about him even if she doubted her late stepmother's account of the marriage.

Since Caro had long ago decided she couldn't trust

her own judgment where men were concerned, she was surprised at the idea that popped into her head after they'd returned home. Maybe she should return to Cliff Walk to make sure Trey Westerly was all right. After all, that first meeting with Jamie had been less than stellar.

After a brief internal argument she left Jamie in the care of their housekeeper, Hannah, and climbed back into her car to return to Cliff Walk. She told herself that it was for Jamie's sake. She needed to explain to Trey about the wide range of his son's problems and how good a chance there was of obliterating them with care and determination. She could also tell him about the need for patience and explain that for a while it might be best to check with her about gifts and activities in order to avert disasters like today's tennis lesson.

But she knew she was lying to herself. She was returning as much for Trey's sake as for Jamie's. Trey drew her. And the defeated, guilty look in his eyes when they'd left just about broke her heart.

Were he not Jamie's long-lost father, she would be even more tempted than she already was to abandon the no-man-in-my-life promise she'd made to herself years ago. He was too handsome. His determination to be a father to his son in this day and age of so many fathers who were nothing more than sperm donors was too compelling. Too touching.

Five minutes after starting out, Caroline stood staring up at the homey Victorian bed-and-breakfast and almost turned around and went back home. Then she heard a loud pinging sound from the other side of Cliff Walk. She easily recognized the sound of tennis balls being smashed against the chain-link fence surrounding the tennis courts. She knew before she even rounded the house that it was Trey. She found him slamming one ball after another into the fence at the back of the empty court. His clear agitation propelled her forward when his thunderous expression should have pushed her away.

Despite the cooling air, sweat had darkened his hair to golden brown and ran in rivulets down his rock-hard jaw. He'd stripped off his jacket and long-sleeved shirt to his white T-shirt, his usual impeccable grooming gone. The muscles of his arms were tense and clearly delineated as he sent the tennis racket into motion time after time, lobbing ball after ball over the net and drilling them into the fence.

She sighed at the sight. Trey Westerly was a hunk and a half. And his frustration level was through the ceiling!

When the bucket was empty, he grabbed it and started scooping up the bright green balls. She couldn't help noticing he had no trouble holding three in each hand before tossing them into the bucket with a little more feeling than they deserved. A few even bounced back out.

"It isn't his fault that they scared him any more than it's theirs," she said, pointing to the bucket of abused balls. Then without another word and before she could talk herself back to her car, Caro entered the court and joined him in his retrieval effort.

"I know it isn't his fault," he said a bit later. He didn't sound the least bit winded but did sound discouraged. "And it isn't yours. But it isn't my fault either. Right?"

There was an odd note in his question, but then he went on talking and picking up the tennis balls and she lost the thought. "Your sister Samantha stopped by and threatened to see me moved into one of the equipment sheds because I'd upset him. I didn't mean to. I just thought we could do something I remember doing with my father." He rounded on her and dropped the bucket. "I've been treated like public enemy number one since I told everyone who I was and I'm sick of it."

"You tried to take my son! How did you expect us to feel toward you? Do you have a clue what being served with those papers did to me? To all of us?"

He dropped to the bench on the sidelines as if his body had lost its starch. "That was never what I wanted. Not really. I came here that first day wanting what the judge gave me and nothing more. But then I saw the way he acted. He seemed so wild and misbehaved so badly, and I thought he needed me full-time. That he needed a father. That I could teach him to control his temper. You could have told me he has this…this weird problem that day."

"The weird problem has a name. SID—Sensory Integration Dysfunction. And I tried to tell you, but you didn't give me a chance to elaborate. You just started criticizing my child and my parenting."

He nodded. "I know. And I apologize. My vision of the son I'd meet here was suddenly and seriously skewed. I was still nearly in shock from learning he even existed. Then…" He grimaced. "We got off on the wrong foot. I'd also like to apologize for the things Charles said in court. He's like a bulldog—or maybe a pit bull."

For some reason having a reasonable conversation made her feel uncertain. She crossed her arms. "Your mother didn't want you to give in the way you did."

"Yes. Well." He looked uncomfortable. "I'm about all she has other than a husband who works too many hours. And Jamie is my son. She's been longing for grandchildren for years. After my disastrous marriage to Natalie, I'm not ever going to marry again. Especially just to indulge Mother's need for a grandchild. Now she's learned that she's had one for years and that she's been denied him."

Caro raised an eyebrow. "And he's going to continue to be if her attitude doesn't change. You were granted visitation. Nothing was said about her. You're going to have to control her if she wants to be more than his grandmother in name only. I won't have her upsetting him."

Anger flared in his eyes, but she saw him rein in his anger, control it. "I'll talk to her. See if I can explain SID better. After I understand it better myself, that is. I got on the Internet yesterday and found some information, but I was just getting into the meat of the site when I was called into a long and difficult surgery. By the time I finished I was practically cross-eyed. This morning I had to get on the road, so I didn't have time. I picked up some things, but my knowledge is still pretty sketchy. He was afraid of the tennis balls, wasn't he?"

She nodded and forced herself to sit down next to him. She leaned back against the chain-link fence, determined to look relaxed even though his nearness put her further on edge.

"I'm confused, though," Trey went on. "He climbed that tree. How could a tennis ball make him flinch like that when he was brave enough to have climbed that tree? There was a stiff breeze that day. Will Reiger and I were terrified."

"Did you get to the part of the Web page that explains the different types of SID? Sensory-avoiding? Sensory-seeking?"

He nodded. "That confused the hell out of me. Which is Jamie?"

"Jamie fluctuates occasionally from sensory-avoiding behaviors to sensory-seeking. It doesn't happen often, but there are those times when he impulsively seeks the stimulation of something he isn't equipped to handle. More often than not he gets hurt when he does and there's little or no warning the switch has happened."

"You mean something he'd usually be afraid to do, like climbing that tree, becomes something he wants to do?"

"Needs to do," she corrected. "And he can just as easily flip back to avoidance. We're lucky he didn't flip while he was up there. The feel of the wind could have overstimulated him, for instance. The thud into your arms may actually have done it. We are supposed to wake Jamie in the morning by rolling him out of bed onto the floor. It sounded pretty cruel to me at first, but apparently it helps integrate the brain."

"So he may want to play tennis someday? And it could happen any day now."

She sighed. How long had she hoped for an instant cure? "Next year or next month or maybe even next week it could click, and he'll start knocking them right back to you. Everything takes patience with Jamie, but then there are these marvelous sudden breakthroughs. He's so bright sometimes it's frightening."

"Isn't anyone teaching him to control himself?"

Caroline guessed this was her chance. "Working with Jamie isn't about control. Get controlling him out of your head. It's about teaching him to understand what he's feeling and how to deal with it or how to make it feel right."

"Tell me about some of his progress," Trey urged. She was struck by the desperate look in his blue eyes. And she instantly understood. It wasn't that there was some mystical connection between them, she told herself. It was only that as one parent to another she understood his need to know there was hope for Jamie to have a normal life—whatever that was.

"He used to shy away from touching anything with more than his fingertips," she told Trey. "Now he can hold almost any object with a firm grasp. Last week he did a finger painting in school. The day before the very idea of touching that paint—the feel of it, the thought of getting it on his hands then having to wash it off— sent him into a tailspin. I can't tell you how proud I was to hang that painting on the refrigerator or how pleased Jamie was to give it to me."

"So I keep trying? Does it get easier?"

"*We* keep trying. And yes it does. Right now you're negotiating a minefield with him." She thought for a moment, remembering those early days when she was on the short end of sanity, never knowing what would set Jamie off next. Caroline suddenly remembered a book she'd found extremely helpful. "I have a book that might help you understand better than any Internet site. It's called *The Out-of-Sync Child*. A lot of parents of SID kids find it very helpful."

"Parent," he said, his voice catching. He cleared his throat. "No one's ever called me a parent before." Trey took a deep breath and blew it out through slightly puckered lips. "I'm not sure I'm ready for that, but I want to be. Believe me, Caroline. I only want what's best for him. I'll read anything you want me to read. I'm sorry about the tennis."

She felt sorry for Trey. He seemed less and less like the ogre Natalie had painted him to be. For some reason admitting that felt dangerous, so she put it away to deal with at another time.

"It was an understandable mistake. I thought there was an outside chance he'd be okay with it. I'd normally take the time to ask his therapists' opinions." She grinned sheepishly. "Someday I'll tell you about our trip to the petting zoo last year. Believe me, this kind of thing happens all the time. For a while maybe you should check with either me or call his therapist directly to see if he has the skill set he needs for an activity you're thinking of sharing with him. The idea is for him to see his own improvement and not feel like a failure all the time. Keeping self-esteem high is very important with these kids because—make no mistake—many are highly intelligent like Jamie and feel failure keenly. The problem is that they might not show it in a way that's acceptable or at first even understandable.

"Also there are certain foods he only gets in moderation. He takes enzyme supplements to help him digest gluten and casein, but we watch how much he gets. It was better than putting him on a restrictive diet. This way he functions in society easier. That's the school's goal—to equip the children for a normal life."

"What other therapies does he get? I know it was all in the court documents, but I'd rather hear it from you."

She fought the urge to smile. He really did see her as Jamie's mother. "Twice a month he sees an osteopathic therapist. The doctor uses techniques that help immeasurably with Jamie, as it seems to with so many SID kids. Then there are the auditory stimulation therapies."

Now he leaned back against the fence. "The CD player?"

She nodded. "We use a method of specially developed CDs. That's what was in his CD player when you first saw him."

"It's an expensive brand. I was surprised to see a seven-year-old with one like that."

"The system uses both sound and music. The quality of the player has to be high. The theory is that receptors in the ear respond to vibration. The therapy can cause vertigo, by the way."

"So when he didn't hear my car, he was really getting therapy, but climbing in those earphones the way he did that first day was even more dangerous than I'd thought."

She hesitated. She couldn't help worrying that she was in many ways training her replacement. But if that were true, for Jamie's sake she still had to do a good job. "Yes and no. He was only listening to music up in the tree. But he was listening to harmonics when he ran in front of your car. And tomorrow Jamie starts hippo therapy."

Trey's eyes widened and their color quite honestly rivaled the bright sky overhead. "Hippo as in *horse?*" he asked.

Distracted by his physical presence and something nearly magical she saw in his gaze, Caroline dragged her attention back to Jamie, where it belonged. She nodded, then found her voice. "The school sponsored a fund-raiser recently and bought a retired show horse. We've been warming Jamie up to the idea of riding Pegasus. He seems ready. Would you like to go watch?"

Trey stared off into the distance, his mind clearly light-years away. "I had a horse once. But then I had to go away to boarding school and Mother sold him. My father bought him for me but then he left us. He paid for his upkeep and care, so he was no bother to Mother, but she called it a bribe. I think she hated that he was a gift from my father and that I loved him."

Goodness, she knew she hadn't liked the woman in court, but now she had more reason than the way she'd acted that day. "She hated that you loved the horse or your father?" she wondered.

Trey's grin was just this side of bitter. "Probably both," he said on a sigh. "I was never so happy as when I was riding—" He stopped midthought and stared at her. His eyes widened. "I'd like to go tomorrow," he said and stood, clearly bothered by either her question or his answer—or as he'd said, probably both.

"Thank you for asking me to tag along," he added, all starchy again, and turned to pick up the rackets and bucket of tennis balls. "I'd better get cleaned up for dinner. Your sister Abigail is the friendly sister, and I'd like to stay on her good side." He moved toward the gate and stopped, turning back. He looked irritated. "You're dangerous, Ms. Hopewell. I hadn't thought about Spirit for years."

And then he walked away as if it was her fault he'd resurrected some sort of painful memory. In Jamie she had one touchy male in her life already. He was enough to handle. She didn't need more.

"So no more getting close to Dr. Prickly!" she muttered and went home.

Chapter Five

Trey's steps quickly ate up the ground between the courts and his room at Cliff Walk. He'd said he was going after a shower and a meal, but what he really sought was a refuge from bitter memories. A refuge from his guilt and from his feelings for Caroline Hopewell.

But though his attraction to her scared the daylights out of him, it was his own feelings he needed to get away from. Not only was he inappropriately drawn to her physically, but emotionally, too. From the start, her beauty had made every hormone in his body sit up and take notice, but he'd been able to control that. Then her obvious love and devotion for Jamie had begun to cool any anger toward her. Now his resolve where she was concerned was weakening dangerously.

Any relationship other than as Jamie's parents was out of the question for them. For the rest of their lives Jamie would tie them together, and Trey was never going to consider another relationship with a woman that wasn't strictly physical and strictly short-term. Caroline wasn't a short-term woman or a short-term presence in his life.

Until she'd returned to the tennis court with comfort in mind, he'd been doing a pretty good job of sticking to the mental off-limits sign he'd posted on her chest during the custody hearing. Now, just because she'd offered a little understanding, he'd found himself revealing a hidden pain from the worst period of his life. His parents' divorce. Losing Spirit was something he'd never talked about. Not even to his father when they'd squared things with each other over the divorce after Trey had turned eighteen.

When he'd first realized he was physically attracted to Caroline, he'd wondered what could be worse. Now he knew. Now he realized they connected emotionally on a plane he hadn't known could exist between a man and a woman. She'd taken him there by instinctively seeing something he'd been hiding from most of his life. Why *had* his mother sold Spirit? Why was it that to love her meant he couldn't love his father equally?

Also battering his emotions was a welling of guilt over Jamie. A puzzle was starting to reveal itself about Jamie's SID, and the connection to him was damned uncomfortable. He'd had to get away before Caroline saw that, as well, but the reprieve would only be temporary. To become acquainted with Jamie, Trey had to spend time with Caroline.

Trey honestly didn't know how he'd fight his multi-level attraction to her. He just knew he had to or Jamie would be caught in the same kind of tug-of-war he'd been when his parents divorced. And since Caroline had invited him along in the morning, he'd better get a hold of himself where she was concerned.

Trey was almost across the foyer of Cliff Walk, headed toward the stairs, when Samantha Hopewell's voice stopped him in his tracks. "Where's the fire, Dr. Westerly?"

He winced and turned toward the doorway that separated the parlor from the large foyer. Samantha stood there in a confrontational stance.

"Sorry. I just didn't want to be late for dinner and add yet another strike against me. I still have time for a shower, right?"

"I wouldn't know. I was just finishing up with the plants." She gestured to the profusion of ferns and other pots in the foyer, then crossed her arms—the picture of belligerence. No matter how friendly Caroline was or how calm Abigail seemed to be about his presence, it was clear this middle sister hated his guts. If he'd had any doubts, when she continued he was sure. "I don't do dinner. Or make the beds. Or dust and vacuum. Neither does Abby. In short, Doctor, we aren't the hired help, and even they aren't here to bow and scrape to the great Wesley Westerly III, M.D. You may have gotten your foot in the door thanks to the judge, but I for one am not giving you an inch."

He honestly didn't know how to deal with such aggressive dislike. "What on earth did Natalie say about me that makes you think I'm the devil incarnate? You

know what? I think I'll just go into town for dinner."
He turned and headed for the front door, but another
voice—soothing and kind—stopped him halfway
across the foyer.

"Dr. Westerly, I apologize for Sam's rudeness."

Trey pivoted back to look at Abigail Hopewell, who
stood behind her still-glaring sister. Abigail, in spite of
her apology, didn't look a whole lot happier. "You have
to understand what your arrival has done. Not only
have you upset my sister and her son—"

"It was never my intention to upset him," he cut in,
"but remember this—he's my son, too."

Abigail took a breath, but her cool brown eyes heated
just a bit for a second before chilling to a new and different brand of control. "Besides frightening and unset-
tling Jamie, you also resurrected the scandal over his
birth. We also heard all about your marriage and the
nightmare it was from Natalie."

"And since your morals are at question, as well as
your fitness as a father and as a human being, know that
we'll all be watching you like a hawk around Jamie,"
Samantha added.

He took a few seconds to absorb the ridiculousness
of the situation. "*My* morals? *Natalie's* version?" His
chuckle was rife with a bitterness he'd thought had
long since evaporated from lack of nourishment. He
studiously tamped it down. Examining it over and over
was unproductive.

"I'm condemned over *Natalie's* version of our marriage? She did what she did and I lack morals? This is
rich! I'm bad for Jamie? You know, I wasn't even going
to mention this because I imagine it was supposed to

be a private moment, but look to your own, ladies. You know what set Jamie off when he climbed that tree last month? He saw your vintner in the barrel room with his hands all over your mother. Hers were pretty busy, as well. Looks to me as if there's just a bit of hypocrisy floating around up here on the cliffs."

He shook his head in disgust and nearly walked away. But he'd never forgive himself if he didn't give their accusations about his marriage to Natalie at least a poke. "You know, I'd love to stick around and hear how Natalie's twisted mind distorted the reality of our life together and my treatment of her, but I just don't think I'd find myself amused. Maybe another day. In the meantime ask yourselves this—who broke up your parents' marriage? Who was it who pawned off another man's child on your father?"

Without another word he whirled around and headed out the door.

Samantha turned toward Abby. "So the tiger once again shows his teeth."

"Sam, all men are not the devil incarnate," Abby responded gently. "Will Reiger, for instance."

Sam grinned. "The same Will who had his hands all over Mama?"

Abby thought about that and grinned, too. Her mother had known Will Reiger for six years. He'd come to Hopewell Vineyards to teach them about wine and growing the grapes to make it. Juliana had been divorced for seven years now. It was time she wasn't alone. Time for her to accept the man who'd been wooing her quietly, slowly, for six years. That would certainly be safe enough. Not impulsive at all. Mama had her passionate nature well in hand. She was Abby's role model. "Mama can take care of herself."

Sam didn't look convinced. "We can but hope. You never know about men. Will included. I'd begun to trust him myself. Now I don't know. Maybe he's had an ulterior motive all these years."

"We should hang a flag. Samantha Hopewell might trust a man! They aren't all liars and cheats and some have extenuating circumstances behind their actions!"

Trey was glad he didn't stay to see how his logical questions were received or what answers either woman might come up with. Forgetting his shower and taking a walking tour of Hopetown did what no outing had in years.

It relaxed him.

As he wandered the streets, admiring the quaint buildings, the river and the view of the steep cliffs across the waterway, Trey became acutely aware that this town was something special. He stood on the bridge between Pennsylvania and New Jersey, staring down at the bubbling water. He watched children toss bread to a flock of geese and wood ducks that floated along, secure in their watery world.

After standing there a while Trey realized his respiration had slowed and his heartbeat had settled into a comfortable rhythm. He looked up in vague surprise at the eclectic town. Not one building matched the others in style or materials. And many sported a riot of colors on their trim, gingerbread accents and the clapboard walls of others.

Busy and disordered though it was, the tranquil nature surrounding it made him feel calm in the face of the storm his life had become. It was then he decided that the place deserved a little exploration. And so he combed through the wide variety of shops and found the shopkeepers as different from one another as their divergent merchandise and clientele.

As he browsed and poked around, he bought gifts for his father and stepmother and his half brothers and sister as well as his mother. The walk had become a shopping spree somewhere along the way.

At a gallery he fell in love with a landscape of the river valley and found himself waiting to have it wrapped in the hope of taking a little peace home with him to the rat race. Sharing the building was a goldsmith so talented Trey found himself asking what the man was doing hidden in Hopetown when New York and Philadelphia were so close. The man's answer, "More isn't necessarily better," had Trey wandering along the road in deep thought.

As he pondered the goldsmith's life truth, Trey came upon a shop that sold a wide-ranging variety of equestrian-related supplies and clothing. He bought a pair of black stone-washed jeans and matching jacket as well as a pair of Western work boots to wear to Jamie's first riding lesson. He hadn't missed Jamie's and Caroline's reaction to his pristine tennis shoes. If he wanted to put Jamie at ease, he had to fit into his son's environment. So on the way to the register he added two more pair of jeans to his purchases.

Trey looked around at the quaint town and knew this was the world where his son belonged and where he wanted him to live. Jamie would only visit his world. And that was how it should be. Not wanting to dwell on reality, however, Trey stopped to eat in a bar, where he munched on French-fried sweet potatoes and enjoyed a beer. Pleasantly tired, Trey looked at his watch and realized it had been years since he'd spent three aimless hours in a row.

And it felt good. He felt good.

Damn good!

He had just reached his car when his cell phone rang. He felt his gut tighten and realized not for the first time exactly what his lifestyle was probably doing to his long-term health. Forcing himself to take a deep, calming breath, he checked the number and happily answered the call from his father.

"Dad," Trey said as soon as he pressed the talk button.

"Couldn't you wait for me to tell you it's me? I swear all these electronic gadgets were invented to make my generation feel old before our time."

Trey grinned. "Hmm…" He pretended to consider the idea. "I find that hard to believe since you're not old and you don't think of yourself as old. I've always wondered if it's still having young kids that keeps you so youthful."

"They aren't kids anymore—at least not the oldest two. I'm getting ready to deal with Susan's junior prom and Griffin's graduation."

Trey unlocked his car and dropped his packages on the backseat while holding the phone between his ear and his shoulder. "And how old is Robert now?"

Wes Westerly laughed. It was a full-throated sound

that always made Trey just a little envious of his father's second family. They'd gotten to hear that sound day in and day out all their lives. He'd had to beg, plead and connive with his mother to get permission for even one weekend a month. His father had fought battle after battle in court till he'd grown tired of the fighting. When Congreve wrote about the fury of hell and a woman scorned, he could have meant Trey's mother in those days. Loss of visitation had been her weapon of choice. Except that battle had left Trey caught in the middle because he was the real weapon.

"Rob's twelve going on twenty," Wes was saying. "He got first prize in the science fair and signed himself up for a geological field trip at the end of July. He may be more mature than Griff at this point. Susan made national merit scholar. I just might not lock her in her room on prom night."

Trey chuckled. "And how is Danielle?"

"Your stepmother was elected president of the garden club. She's over the moon. But enough about me and the rest of mine. How did it go with Jamie? When can we meet our grandson?"

"I don't know when that might be. I'm thinking it may be some time before I have Jamie on my own for any length of time."

"So the mother is still giving you trouble." His father sounded resigned. As if he understood such a thing, and of course he did.

"No. Not really. Although I don't exactly feel welcome here."

"Give her time. I can understand where she's coming from, too. I can remember like it was yesterday how

I felt when your mother ordered me out, then kept you from me. I messed up the marriage, but I was a good father, dammit. Waiting for the courts to rule in my favor that first time was the longest six months of my life."

They'd been Trey's longest, too. He'd gone four of those six months without even a weekend away from school. And that hadn't been the last battle.

"Jamie's adoptive mother is probably still afraid of losing her child," his father went on. "Charles Davenport is a piranha. So was his father. I should know. I had to face him in court time and again just so I could see you."

Guilt weighing him down, Trey walked to a nearby bench and sat. He should never have brought Caroline into court. Even if all he'd seen had been as he'd thought, this was Jamie's world. And now that he'd actually met Jamie and experienced firsthand his son's problems, Trey felt even worse. And not just for jumping to conclusions but also because he'd seen symptoms like Jamie's before. In himself, only to a lesser degree.

"Dad, did you ever think there was something wrong with me?"

"Wrong? Wrong how? Son, not everyone can succeed at their first marriage. I certainly didn't, and you were pretty young to be juggling a wife and med school, then residency."

"No. I mean when I was young. Before you left. After, too."

"Are you talking about you or Jamie? Is there really a problem with him?"

"Oh, I think so. I read a bit on this Sensory Integration Dysfunction before I got here. Caroline explained even more today. Do I remember right? Did I used to rock on the sofa?"

His father chuckled. "And your crib. You rattled the thing apart twice. Drove your mother to distraction. But you were always more content when we left you alone."

Trey felt another piece of the puzzle snick into place. "And do you remember why she clapped me into Abraham Bishop?"

"It wasn't a decision I agreed with, but we were tied up in legal wrangling at the time. She said you'd been misbehaving since I left. Something about being uncontrollable when she took you somewhere."

"I freaked out when the pediatrician swabbed my throat. I can still remember feeling like my brain had short-circuited. Mother called it temper, but I honestly remember not being able to control myself. Thinking I'd lost my mind."

"And Jamie acts like that?"

"Sometimes. Do you remember the way I used to fight about wearing certain clothes? Was terrified of heights? Got sick in cars? And how much time I spent riding Spirit?" He paused. "They're starting Jamie on hippo therapy. *Riding* therapy, Dad. I think maybe I had this SID. I think it's my fault Jamie does."

Dr. Wes Westerly Jr. was a thoughtful man, so silence reigned for a long moment along the wireless highway. "Fault," he said flatly. "I don't think pinning fault for a child's physical problems is constructive or fair. Unless, of course, you purposely coded that boy's DNA so your wife would wind up with a problem child."

Trey chuckled, knowing his father's penchant for making absurd statements to make a point. "It's how I feel."

"Look, Trey, driving you to distraction with her demands was Natalie's fault. Maybe marrying her against Danielle's and my advice makes the failure of your marriage partially your fault. But your child having inherited a learning or behavior problem is just an accident of nature. A *no-fault* accident of birth."

Trey knew all that logically, but knowing and feeling were two different things. Even the bright sunlight couldn't push back the darkness invading his heart and evaporating his good mood. All he had left was a sad, hollow feeling. It felt a lot like failure.

"I can't help feeling like this. Can you imagine what this is like? I thought I'd teach him to play tennis. He was scared spitless of the balls coming at him. He flipped out into a real tantrum, but it was more like an overload. I recognized how he felt, but I didn't have a clue how to help him. He has a lot of symptoms I didn't. He really doesn't like being touched, for instance. God, I can't even hug my son without risking him going off."

"And is there a chance for improvement?"

"Yes. He's apparently already made quite a bit of progress."

"Well, I can tell you this sounds familiar to me, as well."

Trey raked the fingers of his free hand through his hair and let out a breath. "Because it all sounds like me."

"Not all. I meant some of it sounds like my childhood. Just like you, I didn't care to play with other kids. But I never remember feeling lonely. I used to swing on a rope swing in my yard, singing at the top of my lungs for hours. Maybe that's why your rocking never got to me the way it did your mother."

Like father, like son, like grandson. So it *was* his fault. Through what his father called an accident of birth, he'd done this to Jamie.

Chapter Six

Atop Pegasus, Jamie beamed as Trey led him around the ring. The reddish-brown horse seemed huge under her small son, but riding was apparently in his genes. Jamie had taken to Pegasus as if born in the saddle.

And Trey, his golden hair gleaming in the clear, crisp sunlight, had revealed a surprising love of horses. Caroline was beginning to think she was seeing the real Trey minus the pressure-driven career. Just being near the big animal seemed to relax him. And not just that, but it gave him an almost tangible link of his own to Jamie.

That was a good thing, she told herself. Jamie and Trey needed to find common ground and they had. It hadn't taken her long to see that. It was like magic watching them circle the ring, sharing this moment. Enjoying it together.

Pegasus butted Trey in the middle of his back with his big head, knocking him forward, and her son's laughter floated across the ring toward her on a crisp spring breeze. She felt a helpless grin tip her lips when Jamie shouted, "Yeah. Faster."

Trey turned and walked backward, facing boy and horse. Obviously pretending to be disgruntled, he said something to the horse in a low voice, coaxing another peal of laughter from Jamie. Then Trey turned and picked up the pace, giving Jamie pointers on how to move with the horse's quickened pace and making Alan Smith, the trainer, look more than a little superfluous as he stood on the sidelines. The older man, however, seemed to be enjoying the show as much as the players.

Caro had been mildly surprised earlier this morning when they had met Trey outside Cliff Walk wearing a black Hopetown T-shirt, jeans and a black denim jacket to match. But the newness of them and his boots explained where he'd been at dinner last night. When she'd seen him, she'd given him immediate points for trying to dress down for the day's activities, thinking she'd misjudged his ability to adapt. Now she had to wonder if she hadn't misjudged him about a lot of things.

"That's enough for today," Alan Smith called out, approaching Trey and Jamie after an hour. Had he not ended the session, Caroline thought Trey would have gladly led the big, lumbering old hunter around that ring all day.

Trey stopped and turned to the man, smiling. "Have we really been at this an hour?"

Jamie stiffened. "No. I want to ride." He rocked and kicked his feet. "Go," he shouted. "Go."

Snorting, the horse sidestepped nervously and Jamie's eyes widened. He froze. She knew it was a look of fear her son wore. It was apparent Trey did, too. He quickly handed the reins to the instructor and turned toward Jamie, talking in a soothing tone. Unfortunately during the transfer of the reins, Pegasus started to rise up on his hind legs.

Trey moved like lightning then, snatching Jamie out of the air when he flew out of the saddle and carried him across the ring, away from the danger of the upset animal. Caroline hurried over and opened the gate, allowing them through, then securing it after them.

She whirled back, intent on rushing to her son's side, wanting to comfort him. Trey already had set Jamie on the ground and was on one knee in front of Jamie so that they were eye to eye. Rather than explode in a torrent of emotions as they both expected, Jamie stared wide-eyed at Trey.

"Jamie," he admonished before the scream she could see rising from Jamie's small chest could fully form, "look at how scared Pegasus is now."

Jamie sucked in a startled breath and his eyes flicked toward the pawing, quivering horse. "Scared?" he asked in a slightly squeaking voice. Brow crinkled in confusion, he stared at Pegasus thoughtfully for a long moment.

Gilt hair rustling in the stiff breeze, Trey was clearly reaching for patience and calm. Finally, when Jamie looked back at him, Trey nodded. "Yes. Scared. Just because he's big doesn't mean he can't be afraid. There are a lot of things in this world that frighten Pegasus because he doesn't understand them. There are other things he does understand. He understands gentle treatment. A soft, firm command. He understands the signals that tell him what to do. The feel of your heels against his side, your movements and the position of the reins tell how and where you want him to go. Remember Mr. Smith started out teaching you those signals?"

Jamie nodded effusively. "I wanted him to go! I didn't want to stop," he said stubbornly. "I liked it. I really did!"

Trey just looked at him with a raised eyebrow. "I think we all know that. But Mr. Smith told you how to make him start ahead and how to stop him. Pegasus got riled up because we were telling him two different things to do. I was telling him to stop because Mr. Smith said our hour was up. You were saying go ahead. Then you kicked and that told Pegasus to run. It mixed up all his feelings and he didn't know what to do with them."

Jamie frowned thoughtfully. "That happens to me a lot."

Trey sighed quietly. "I know. You don't like it, do you?"

Frown still in place, Jamie said, "No. And I can't make it stop."

"Neither can Pegasus. You have to promise to never do that again or you won't be allowed to ride. I know you don't want that to happen, do you?"

Jamie scowled, glanced at the horse being led into the stable and shook his head.

"Then from now on when it's time to stop, we have to stop. Deal?" Trey stuck out his hand.

Jamie seemed to consider his options. Then he put his hand in Trey's and they shook hands. Caro blinked away a tear. Trey was learning quickly, instinctively.

Jamie looked up at her. "Can I tell Pegasus I'm sorry and then can we go to the river, Mama?"

Glad she'd thought of that ahead of time, Caro forced a grin and told him, "Isn't that a coincidence? I just happen to have hidden a picnic hamper in the trunk of Trey's car while he was finishing his breakfast."

"Yea!" Jamie grabbed for her and started pulling her toward the car.

Caro glanced at Trey, who looked so isolated suddenly it made her heart ache. She could almost see a mantle of reticence descend on him. For a little while he'd seemed to step outside himself and was able to find just the right thing to say to Jamie. Then she realized he didn't know he was invited.

As her mother had wisely pointed out to her and her sisters, Trey was in Jamie's life to stay. It was her job to be there during these early days of their relationship and help them learn how to deal with each other, no matter how uncomfortable her attraction to Trey made her feel. She would be wrong not to help negotiate a path between them.

"There's plenty," she told Trey. "I thought you'd like to see Jamie's favorite spot along the river. We have to drive there."

He looked surprised but covered the confused look in his eyes quickly. "I'd love to come. Is that okay with you, Jamie?" he asked.

Jamie frowned, but in thoughtfulness not disagreement. "Sure. I-If you want."

"Of course I want. Very much, son. I'm only here to spend time with you. We have seven years to catch up on and I'd hate to waste another second."

"You aren't mad at me 'cause I scared Pegasus?"

"I was concerned for both you and the horse. I'm your father, Jamie. I'd never get so angry with you that I wouldn't want to be with you, any more than your mother would. I'd like us to get to know each other better so you'll be sure of that."

It was a ten-minute ride between the riding academy and their special spot on the river. Jamie rode in the backseat wearing his headphones and bouncing and rocking as much as the seat belt allowed. Jamie aboard her SUV was one thing, but in Trey's small, sporty midsize it was another thing altogether. At one red light he had the whole car rocking. Trey's jaw was rock-hard when she glanced at him.

"I can tell him to stop," she ventured.

"If he didn't need to rock, he wouldn't, right?"

"I've noticed when he's told to sit still in a car he gets motion sick, but if it bothers you—"

"It doesn't bother me," Trey said, but it came out short and tense, belying his denial. *His mood isn't affecting Jamie,* she decided. So she dropped it, telling herself his inner turmoil was none of her business. It was a short ride, after all, and he was the adult.

They drove along the road next to the canal until just after it merged with the river. The day warmed and the sun continued to shine, playing peekaboo from behind high, fluffy clouds. Their special spot was far enough off the beaten path that tourists rarely strayed there. The important thing about it was that it wasn't on Hopewell property, so to Jamie being there was always an adventure.

She directed Trey off the road and through a short tunnel of trees, where they parked under the heavily leafed canopy. The white flowers of the wild dogwoods provided a contrast to the bright spring green of the surrounding woodlands. Jamie carried the blanket, bouncing along next to Trey, who carried the picnic hamper for the short walk to the grassy bank of the river.

Caroline stayed back a bit, watching them. They looked so much like father and son that it made her heart ache just a bit. Trey's hair, a darker shade of deep gold, was a preview of where Jamie's color was headed. Both were tall, though Jamie's height was relative to his age, and both had the same rangy build and walk. Again, looking at Trey was like a peek into the future. Jamie seemed happy as he pointed out various points of a seven-year-old's interest, and Trey nicely pretended to be suitably impressed.

"Mama, can I swing?" Jamie called to her, pointing to the rustic old rope swing they'd found there the first time they found the spot.

"After we eat," she promised and watched Trey take the heavy blanket from Jamie and spread it out about twenty feet from the gurgling river.

"Can I feed the ducks?" Jamie begged.

"After we eat," she said again. "Hannah packed all your favorites. Fried chicken strips, applesauce and carrot salad and custard pie."

"It sounds as if we have something else in common, Jamie," Trey said, placing the hamper in the center of the blanket. "I love fried chicken and applesauce, too. I don't think I've had the others, but if Hannah is as good at salad and pie as she is at pancakes, I will."

And he did. Both he and Jamie brought hearty appetites with them to the meal. No sooner had he finished than Jamie was bouncing up and demanding attention. "I'm feedin' the ducks now. Where's the bread? Did Hannah send my duck bread?"

Trey leaned back on his elbows, crossing his legs at the ankles, and grinned. "Duck bread?" he asked.

That grin had her stomach bouncing as much as Jamie's feet were. "Bread that's too dry to eat but too good to throw out," she explained as she pulled the bag out of the hamper to distract herself. She handed it to Trey and their hands touched. Both of them yanked their hands back and the bread fell between. Embarrassed, Caro looked away, tossing her hair off her cheek, hoping to cover the gaffe.

Trey picked up the bread and looked it over. "Ah. Of course. How foolish of me not to know all about duck bread." It was said so smoothly she was sure she'd imagined that he'd been partly to blame for creating the awkward moment.

"Uh-uh. I made it up!" Jamie squealed and let out a belly laugh as if he'd told the funniest joke ever.

"Well. There you go," Trey said and chuckled, but the shining look in his eyes said his mirth was because he'd finally gotten to experience the real Jamie. "That makes you smarter than the average seven-year-old in my book any day of the week." Trey looked toward her. "Do you want me to walk down to the water with him while you pack up here?"

It was hard to say yes. This had been their spot—hers and Jamie's—until now. Duck feeding was their ritual.

Trey clearly noticed her reticence. "Or I could pack up. Or we could let the ants have a feast and take him down together," Trey suggested.

Caroline was determined not to give in to petty urges. She shook her head. "No. Go ahead. He's leery of the water, but still be careful he doesn't trip and fall in. Teaching him to swim hasn't been possible yet."

Trey nodded. "So, Jamie, what do you say we get started making sure Daffy and Daisy Duck and all their cousins have their lunch?" He held out his hand and Caro could see how much he wanted Jamie to take it.

"Donald. It's Donald and Daisy Duck," Jamie corrected as he put his small hand into Trey's. Trey blinked, clearly almost overcome, and they walked toward the river. He glanced back at her and Caroline knew it was gratitude she read in his gaze.

Caroline was ashamed because all she could think as she looked away from his compelling gaze and went back to her task was that she wished none of them had ever lain eyes on him.

His heart lighter than it had been in years, Trey rolled up the now-empty bread wrapper. "I guess they've deserted us," he said and slid to the ground off the big, sun-warmed rock on the bank. Chuckling, Caroline got to her feet, too, at the far side of the boulder. She'd joined them sometime after he and Jamie had successfully lured the ducks toward the bank with the promise of a meal. He'd been surprised at how glad he'd been to have Caroline there with them and at how incomplete the experience had seemed till she'd joined them.

His mother seemed to think Caroline's presence would intrude on his time with Jamie. He'd wondered if it might but had initially gone along with Juliana Hopewell's plan for Jamie's sake. Trey had to admit that in a way his mother was right—but in a different, more perilous fashion. He was attracted to Caroline in a way he had never been to any other woman. Like that moment with the bread. He'd tried to cover his ridiculous reaction to her electric touch but feared he'd failed. Luckily Jamie had provided a distraction at the perfect time. And there were those other moments when they made eye contact and her gaze acted on him like a paralyzing drug.

In more ways, however, he was glad Caroline was around. She was a tremendous help in making Jamie comfortable around him. She was able to fill in silences that might become awkward, because she knew his son so much better then he did.

The fact was that though they were virtual strangers, they were partners in parenthood and she was an invaluable help. Thanks to her, Jamie was beginning to relax with him. They'd all laughed a great deal at the flock of ducks. The birds had been happy in each other's company only minutes before the arrival of food. But when presented with a meal, they'd pecked and squabbled with each other, vying for greater and greater portions of the booty. Now the flock was back to their tranquil selves, floating placidly upstream.

"There they go. Just like always, right, Jamie?" Caroline said. "Off to beg another meal farther upstream."

"And now it's swing time," Jamie called over his shoulder as he scrambled off their rocky perch and tore off toward an old, wooden-seated rope swing that hung from a tall branch not far from the water's edge.

"That means we can rest," Caroline sighed happily.

"We don't need to push him?" he said unnecessarily, since Jamie already had the swing moving back and forth. CD headphones in place, Jamie appeared to be in heaven.

His son had a beautiful smile. Trey glanced at Caroline. And so did his son's mother.

"He's been pumping for himself since he was four," she explained. "That way he only goes as high as he feels comfortable with. He gets himself higher and higher all the time. Actually he's about maxed out on that swing."

"He's afraid of heights," Trey translated. That was a problem he'd actually had to go for therapy in his twenties to get over. Did the parallels never end? On the ride over there Jamie had reminded him of himself with his rocking. The motion honestly hadn't bothered him, as he knew Caroline thought. What it had done was heap on more guilt and bring back painful memories of his parents arguing because of his rocking. He'd always known he'd put so great a strain on his parents' marriage that the divorce had been his fault.

Trey glanced at Caroline and found he longed to talk out his guilty feelings with her. To tell her he understood Jamie more than she might think. But, right or wrong, he was ashamed. Her life with Jamie and Jamie's life itself was so much harder than it would have been had Trey not been Jamie's father. He just couldn't bring himself to admit it to her.

His mother's voice, sharp and shaken, rose in his mind. *I'm ashamed of you, Wesley. How could you embarrass me that way?* How many times had she said that or a variation of it, leading to the day she'd taken him to the Academy and left him there to learn not to be such a little animal? The Abraham Bishop Academy had taught him one important thing. Control. Iron control. He'd never heard her or anyone say anything like that again, but now he knew that lesson had not needed to be nearly as painful.

"Really he's not all that afraid of heights anymore," Caroline said, breaking into his speeding thoughts. "Even though he was in a sensory-seeking period, I don't think he would have climbed that tree if he was as shy of heights as he once was. Four years ago sitting atop Pegasus would have terrified him. That was the problem that sent me to a psychologist for him at such a young age. We went into a glass-enclosed elevator and he utterly panicked. The gradual therapies have helped that most of all."

The tension Trey had been feeling since learning of Jamie's problem eased a bit. Jamie's journey to what most people called normal was going to be less painful than his had been. His son was being led slowly through the maze of his haywire sensitivities in a way that wouldn't leave him scarred and guilt-ridden. No one treated Jamie as he had been treated—like a demon child who'd made his mother rethink having more children.

That his mother was so alone weighed heavily on Trey because he knew that was his fault, too. Was it any wonder she focused so much on him? Because of him she had no other children to lean on, worry about, care about. Therefore he'd always keenly felt his duty to her. It was his responsibility to help fill the void she felt now in her later years.

He'd call her tomorrow. She'd done her best by him, he told himself, trying not to resent her inability to deal with him the way Caroline did Jamie. He told himself that even Caroline admitted Jamie's problem was so newly discovered and understood that many health and educational professionals still saw it as ADHD. But Trey remembered his own out-of-control, short-circuited, haywire feelings.

He knew SID was real.

He also knew that only Caroline's diligence had uncovered the right diagnosis even in a world resistant to these new insights. "Thank you," he said, looking at her as she smiled and watched Jamie intently.

She looked away from their son to him. "You mean for including you in our picnic? How else am I going to be able to make sure you two get off on the right foot? Look, Trey, I'm doing this for Jamie. I selfishly still wish I'd left Jamie out of the ribbon-cutting ceremony that day. I wish I could go back and have him all to myself again. But I can't, so I'm doing what's best for Jamie."

Wincing inwardly at her honesty, Trey forced himself to explain his meaning. "But that's what I mean. You've done so much for him. I haven't seen the school or how it operates, but I know you do everything you do with him in mind. You sought out and found an obscure diagnosis with difficult and troublesome therapies. And you've done them. You've gone the extra mile to see that my child has the life he deserves."

She tilted her head and studied him with slightly narrowed eyes. "He's my child, too, Trey. I love Jamie. Of course I went the extra mile for him. Statistics on these kids untreated are frightening. There are several studies that link delinquency and drug abuse and self-destructive behavior with untreated learning disabilities. I couldn't sit back and do nothing. I had to find out what was wrong and try to help him any way I could."

"You didn't have to. It hasn't escaped my notice that you could have just let him become a ward of the state when your father and Nat were killed."

She blinked. "Too late. I loved him already. And as far as I was concerned, he *had* a family. He was my half brother. Since I never intend to marry, Jamie gave me the chance to be a mother that I'd never have otherwise. Now that I know he doesn't have a drop of Hopewell blood, I still love him like a son."

"Well, for what it's worth, I'm glad he has you."

Caroline's eyes widened. She was clearly surprised by his endorsement. Her big green eyes filled with tears then and she bit her lip, looking toward Jamie for a long moment. Trey studied her. A beautiful woman, with a creamy complexion, a finely drawn nose and full, soft-looking lips, who seemed determined to have nothing in her life but a fledgling business and a child she poured all her emotional energy into. By her own admission she never intended to marry. He knew she must have her reasons, as he had his, but she reminded him of a princess who stayed inside her castle taking care of those who depended on her but was afraid to venture outside the gates.

"But me being in his life means that you'd still have

missed the last seven years," she said after a long pause. He nodded. "Then I guess it's my turn to thank you for the vote of confidence," she said.

Trey found it hard to look away, until Jamie screamed, "Mama! It's breaking."

Trey looked up and saw what Jamie must have. He was swinging at the optimum height for the old swing, and the weathered hemp rope now hung from the branch by a single thread. Jumping to his feet, Trey ran and plucked Jamie from the swing just as the rope broke and the swing's seat fell from beneath him. The boy tumbled into Trey's chest, his long, thin arms wrapping around his neck.

It was a little bit of heaven and hell to feel his child so close but to still wait for an explosion of fear or anger because he was being held. Trey braced himself, waiting for Jamie to frantically push away, but instead a giggle gurgled next to his ear. His heart turned over at the sound.

"You caught me!" Jamie said, his voice full of awe. "You always catch me now."

Trey hadn't known a heart could break from an overload of joy, but that quiet day by the burbling river he learned it could happen. And he was grateful for the pain.

Chapter Seven

The noonday sun warmed the second-floor balcony of Bella Villa, their Tuscan-inspired banquet facility. Caroline braced her hands on the wall and watched Trey and Jamie on the hillside below, hard at a game of hide-and-seek among the vines. The spring breeze stirred the handkerchief hem of her skirt against her calves and her hair against her cheeks. The river beyond and far below them twisted and turned between the high cliffs—a shining, fluid ribbon that bordered two states. She would never have thought the relationship between father and son would have progressed so quickly and so well when Trey arrived a week ago with a bucket of tennis balls and dreams far beyond Jamie's current capabilities.

Other movement off in the eastern field drew her attention. Her mother and Will strolled along in the shadow of the vines. "There's something going on between those two," she told Abby and Sam, who were sipping tea and critiquing Abby's latest brochure.

Both her sisters turned in their chairs to look out over the fields, following her gaze to their mother. "I never thought Will would do anything about his feelings," Samantha said.

"I'm glad he finally is," Abby mused quietly. "Six years may have seemed like a long time to heal, but Mama wasn't ready till now—if she even is yet. Natalie destroyed her whole world except for us. It's time she took a little happiness for herself."

Sam rolled her eyes at Caroline. Samantha's opinion on who was at fault in the divorce and its surrounding scandal hadn't been in doubt from the first day. She blamed their father.

Before a debate detoured them hopelessly off the subject at hand, Caro reminded both her sisters of the troubled waters ahead. "Will's been lying about who he really is for all of those six years, and Mama is particularly sensitive to lies. I worry about what she'll do when she finds out he's half owner of Old Country Wines." Caro sat down, picking up her cup. She took a sip of the good, strong tea, then went on. "She could toss him out on his ear."

"At least we can tell her Will confessed to us two years ago," Sam reminded them. "And he was just trying to help her the only way he thought she would let him."

"Pretending to be an Old Country employee *was* the only way," Abby said. "Mama really does mistrust wealthy men because of the way Father treated her."

Trying to enjoy the sun-warmed breeze of the May day, Caroline followed the two figures with her gaze as they checked the budding vines on the hillside below. "I just wish he hadn't involved us. That's the last time I agree to keep someone's secret before I know what it is," she said absently, watching as Will settled his arm across her mother's shoulders. "So tell me. What did Will say about lending us the payment?"

Sam was closest to Will, so she'd been elected to ask. "He can't," Sam told them now. "He said he'd even be willing to risk telling Mama about who he is. But his brother just started an expansion of Old Country's facility and they're cash-poor right now themselves. He could help out in a couple of months, but we could solve our own problems by then."

Caro nodded, disappointed, but accepted the outcome. Will had taught them everything he knew about the wine business and in the process had become like a father to her and her sisters. And he was a good deal better than the one life had dealt them. If there was a way to help, Will would have found it.

"He even went to talk to Harley Bryant at the bank yesterday," Sam reported. "Harley wouldn't talk to him about an extension."

Caroline hated to even think about that loan, considering all the pressure she was under over Jamie, but the next payment loomed ever closer. And what was frustrating was that they were so near to being able to pay that she could smell it. So near yet so, so far. All they needed was a four-month extension. But for some reason the bank was being difficult. She'd made every balloon payment on time until now so, practically speaking, the refusal made little sense. It was as if Harley Bryant—bank president and majority stock-holder—had a grudge against them.

A big one.

The problems with their finances had arisen because Harley Bryant, who also currently held the position of Hopetown's mayor, had engineered several roadblocks that had slowed the construction of Bella Villa and the renovation of Cliff Walk. The opening of both new legs of their business had been held up a full year. And therefore they were a year behind in expected profits. Unfortunately the proceeds from the fall/winter sales cycle wouldn't begin to flow in until four months after the loan payment came due.

She'd tried to negotiate. She'd even gone to other banks, but she'd been turned down as a credit risk. Caroline was in the process of trying to clear a phantom blotch that had appeared on the winery's credit and was stopping her from negotiating another loan. Unfortunately it was taking too long and the payment was nearly due.

The crux of the matter was that Harley Bryant's actions made no sense. They could easily prove he'd manufactured the situation—possibly even the credit problems. If he meant to call the loan and try taking the winery, they could in all likelihood tie it up in court long enough to come up with the money. But she knew that would hurt business and truly hurt their credit.

"I'm going to go see Harley today to see if I can give him a gentle nudge toward being more reasonable," Caro told her sisters.

Abby put her cup down a little harder than necessary.

"I'd like to give him a good hard shove myself!" she said through gritted teeth, then sucked in a startled breath. Her eyes widened before she closed them and took a slow, deep breath. After regaining her near-legendary composure, she said, "Do you think Harley's angry about my letters to the editor? He almost lost the election because of the negative sentiment I caused toward his plans to homogenize the buildings in town. The talk in town is that he'll be lucky to get elected dog catcher next go-round."

"We'll deal with it no matter what the cause," Caroline said and lifted her cup as if to propose a toast. "Politicians should be ready for constituents to disagree with them."

"You'd think so, wouldn't you? What I don't understand is if not the letters, why is he doing this?"

"I don't guess it really matters," Sam said and raised her cup, the light of grim determination in her eyes. "Here's to beating him at his own game. And somehow we will. To Mama's dream and keeping it alive."

All three sisters gladly joined in on the toast. After clicking cups, they turned as one to watch romance bud along with the vines.

It was going on three when Caroline unlocked her car and slid inside. In a daze she gripped the wheel and rested her forehead on the back of her hands. How could such a lovely day turn so bad? And what was Harley Bryant up to?

The man had actually stared at her as if she'd lost her mind when she'd accused him of being unreasonable and of holding a grudge against the family. He'd sat a bit straighter then and called her unprofessional for expecting any more special treatment. He'd loaned her mother the start-up capital when no one else would touch her. Because he'd been a friend of James Hopewell's, he'd loaned them a small fortune. That was special treatment enough.

Then he'd really lowered the boom. It was, he'd said, time the Hopewells learned the hard facts of business. If the payment wasn't on time, his bank intended to call the loan. Her stomach skittered again.

They now stood to lose their livelihood—their dream.

Sitting up, Caro dropped her head back on the headrest for a second, then started for home. They still had time. She'd think of something. She had to.

Determined to take back the day, Caro rolled the windows down and tore out the pins that held her hair in a neat little chignon. Hair flying in the breeze, she zipped along the winding river road from town in her mother's game little Mercedes. Even seven years after her father had given it to her mother as part of the divorce settlement, the little car purred like a tamed mountain lion.

But the speed and the wind didn't do their usual job of calming her down, so she sped by Hopewell Manor, not yet ready to plaster on a brave face. A mile and a half later the entrance to the vineyard campus yawned ahead. Still unable to face questions that had no answers, she drove on, racking her brain for a plan.

As if drawn by some invisible force, she found herself pulling off the road and travelling down the short gravel path to her and Jamie's special spot by the river.

When she noticed Trey's low-slung car parked there, Caro nearly backed up, but then she realized what he was doing and felt compelled to stay.

To thank him.

What was it, she wondered as she leaned against his car to watch him, that made a man doing physical work so darn sexy and irresistible?

Trey was so intent on his task that he didn't notice her until she called his name. Then in one fluid motion he stopped and looked back over his shoulder, surprise and a bit of consternation written on his features. "Caroline, I thought you had a meeting?"

She huffed out a breath. "Could we talk about anything but that meeting? Like what you're up to?" Caro wondered what his mother would say if she could see him in his blue jeans and a Hopetown Does It Slowly T-shirt. The stiff and starchy Marilyn Guilford would probably be horrified.

Trey propped a hand on his hip and grinned. "I thought I could rehang the swing. I went and bought nylon climbing rope in town. All I have to do is get it over that branch." He pointed high up in the tree.

"But the other swing hung off that lower branch. Wouldn't that be easier?"

"Probably, but the old one looked to be at its optimum swinging height. If I can get it up and over that higher branch, it'll be more fun for Jamie when he wants to go higher and that way he can get used to heights on his own terms."

She smiled. "You're reading the book."

"There wasn't much else to do last night after Jamie left," he said with a shrug. "Besides, I'd read a hundred books if I could understand better and help him." He turned away as if embarrassed and gave the rock he'd tied with the rope another toss. This time it looped neatly over the high branch. "Yes!" he called out. "Now when he goes into one of those sensory-seeking periods this'll be here for him. A swing has to be better than climbing a tree."

"On those occasions when you aren't here to catch him," she finished and smiled, remembering Trey's expression yesterday when Jamie popped up with that comment. "He really got you with that one, didn't he?"

Trey nodded as he tied two ropes to the one that he'd tossed over the branch. "Good description. I was afraid he'd never accept me after the way he acted Monday. Now it's only Wednesday and he hugged me good night last night. If the kid ever calls me Daddy, I'll probably melt into a puddle at his feet."

The thought of them growing close worried her—for her sake and Jamie's, too. He didn't seem to be the man Natalie had described, but how could she know for sure? Anyone could pretend for a few days. "Jamie has a big heart, Trey." She was tempted to add, *Just don't break it,* but she thought better of it. Caroline knew herself well enough to know that she didn't have the energy for another confrontation after her showdown with Harley Bryant. She still didn't know how she was going to tell her family how badly she'd failed them.

"What's wrong?" Trey asked, the tone of concern in his voice unmistakable.

Caroline's vision cleared and she realized she'd been staring off into space. "Wrong?"

"I don't know you well, Caroline, but you honestly

look as if you've lost your last friend. Look, I told you I have no intention of suing for custody, if that's what has you so worried. Jamie should grow up here. This is a nice area. The town is wonderful and friendly. There are all these wide-open spaces with the educational possibilities of a big city not far away. And most important, you are a wonderful mother."

Caroline smiled softly, his words dampened by the fear for the winery. "Thank you," she said simply. She allowed herself to bask in his praise for a brief minute before settling for reality. "But Jamie isn't the problem. I had some bad news. Bad *business* news," she added. "I just don't know how to tell my family. But, of course, I have to." She didn't know how it happened, but she found herself sinking onto a fallen log and spilling out the whole seemingly impossible financial problem the Hopewells found themselves in.

Trey leaned against the hood of his car, experiencing a deluge of guilt as she explained the situation. He couldn't have picked a worse time to storm into her life. Listening to her story made him furious. Hadn't these four women endured enough heartache and disappointment?

He'd thumbed through the scrapbooks in Cliff Walk's dayroom and had been surprised by how far they'd come in six years. They'd turned what had once been a parcel of useless land atop a rocky promontory that overlooked the river valley below into a thriving vineyard.

A derelict house that had been within spitting distance of a wrecking ball was now Cliff Walk, a museum-quality renovation of Victorian elegance. And from what he'd overheard, business at Bella Vista promised to be brisk in the future.

"So you're shy on the loan payment and he's going to call the whole thing in if you don't come up with it on time?" he asked.

"And Harley won't take our promised orders as a guarantee of payment. Pardon the vineyard pun, but he has us over a barrel."

It sounded as if Harley Bryant really did have them over a barrel. Something about that word sparked a distant memory. Barrel. Barrel futures!

"I'm not much of a businessman, but had you thought of doing what the big California wineries do? Sell futures?"

Caro looked at him, giving him a small smile. "The operative word is *big*. We'll never be that big."

"Hmm." Trey turned his head, considering. "Is there some kind of rule against a small winery doing it?"

Caroline frowned, deep in thought. She slowly shook her head. "No, but they usually offer futures after barrel-tasting events. The California wineries even sponsor food-and-wine festivals that draw huge crowds. We don't get all that much traffic this far from Hopetown. We're into our busier time of the year till late fall but…but…" She stopped, her eyes going from tired jade to sparkling emerald. "Abby talked about the idea of holding a big event right here using all our facilities so people would see how beautiful Bella Villa is." Caro jumped up from the log and began pacing. "I thought of inviting artisans and specialty-foods vendors to occupy booths that we would rent out. Wine lovers would like the shopping opportunity and maybe buy some futures."

"Maybe the resort owners from the Poconos you rely on would enjoy the weekend and maybe they could be persuaded to go for them, too," Trey suggested.

Caroline pivoted toward him. "And maybe we could invite the general managers of the big Philadelphia hotels. We've been trying to get them to use us as a house wine. The GMs from the Atlantic City casino hotels, too."

He thought of all the interest he'd noticed in Hopewell Manor. "Could you offer tours of your house? Several of the tourists I've met have asked about the inside of the manor."

She couldn't fight a grin. "People are *always* asking to see inside. Of course, that would have my grandmother spinning in her grave."

Trey winced. "Then maybe you should forget that part."

Caroline chuckled. "Did I tell you none of us ever liked my grandmother?"

"There you go then. Could you get it together soon enough to help with the payment?"

"It could work. I really think it could!" Caroline stopped pacing. She was almost vibrating with excitement. He knew there was no blood relation between her and Jamie, but that was who she reminded him of at that moment. It made sense because he'd always thought children drew equally from environment and genetics. "But only if we get the PR and invitations out soon enough," she went on, reaching for her cell phone. "I have to go. We have to get on this. Get organized. Thank you! Thank you," she said, then stretched toward him.

Trey was sure she meant to drop a light kiss on his cheek but... Hadn't he been wondering for days how her lips would taste?

Timing being everything in life, Trey turned his face to hers. He was sure sometime in the future he'd agree that it was worth every electric, confusing, mind-warping second. But right then he lost the ability to think a single coherent thought.

As if of their own accord, his lips clung to hers, taking the moment further—longer than he'd planned. Of course he hadn't planned this at all. One didn't plan a hurricane, a tornado or a tidal wave of emotion such as this. And what was scarier than losing his iron grip was that he didn't think she had any more control over those thrilling, terrifying moments than he did.

What am I doing? he thought as his hands moved to her shoulders. *Push her away!* he ordered himself.

But his body. Oh, his body had other ideas, and he deepened the scrumptious kiss. His tongue wanted more of her sweet taste. His senses drove him forward as he took a deep breath, dragging in her scent—something that rivaled the aroma of the spring that surrounded them. Then his hands demanded their own reward and nearly took it as they sought out those soft, small mounds that had been teasing him, tempting him, for days.

Then his mind—or hers—won the silent battle for restraint and she moved away. Blinking up at him, she whispered, "I...we...that wasn't..."

He pressed his fingertips against her slightly swollen lips. "A good idea. Yeah. I know. Maybe you'd better go before I change my mind about letting you leave."

He smiled at the slightly perplexed look on her beautiful face. "You were off to plot against the town's evil banker with Abby and Samantha."

Caroline blinked. "Oh. Right. I'd better go." And she did. With haste. *Which is a good thing,* he thought as he fought the temptation to follow her to her car.

Chapter Eight

"You're out of your mind," Caroline told her reflection as she got ready for dinner. The mirror didn't lie. Her eyes were too bright. Her hands weren't steady. She'd not only kissed Trey Westerly but it felt as if electricity coursed through her veins just because he'd be at dinner. Caro tossed down the brush she didn't remember picking up. Determined to stop fussing with her hair, she stepped back and fretted over her emerald silk slack set instead. Maybe it was too much for a family dinner.

She should change.

No, this was a special dinner. A thank-you dinner. They would all be dressed up. Well, except for Sam, but Sam didn't abandon her jeans for anyone or anything. And Abby was still working on the festival plans when she'd left her at her office in Cliff Walk.

If Abby and Sam weren't dressed as fancy as she was, it might look as if she'd gone to a lot of trouble. Which she had, but only because what she'd been wearing had been wrinkled, she assured herself. It had absolutely nothing to do with Trey. Nothing.

"You know," she told her reflection. "You truly are certifiable." Accepting that much as true, Caroline forced herself to turn away from the mirror. As she did, she paused and glanced around her azure-blue sanctuary. This room, hers from childhood, with its silk draperies, creamy Abusson carpet and warm cherry furniture, had always brought her to a calm place. Tonight it had failed—miserably. She dropped onto the edge of her sleigh bed and closed her eyes, remembering what had gotten her into this mess.

The idea Trey had sparked.

She wasn't sorry about that, of course. She'd been thrilled with the chance to get off the treadmill Harley Bryant's inflexibility and machinations had put them on. Caro was now convinced that Harley must have been after the winery from the beginning. As their banker, he knew their business plan. Which meant he'd known from day one that they'd be counting on the proceeds from the B and B and the banquet facility to make this quarter's payment. As mayor and president of the zoning board in the name of preserving Hopetown's way of life, he'd tossed up one roadblock after another, causing a significant one-year's delay in opening Bella Villa.

Caroline's problem now was that, to thank Trey for his thought on selling futures, her mother had insisted he be invited for dinner. Her reticence had nothing to do with Jamie, but she couldn't exactly tell her family that Trey had been thanked way too much already, could she? She certainly couldn't explain exactly how she'd endeavored to thank him or that she was embarrassed because a friendly thank-you peck on the cheek had become a passionate kiss.

And of course Trey hadn't let a little thing like kissing her stop him from spending even one minute with Jamie. He'd readily accepted the invitation, proving the kiss hadn't meant a thing to him. He was a typical man—damn him!

Even though she didn't like it, Caro couldn't blame Juliana and Abby for wanting to thank Trey for the idea that had sparked the flurry of activity and planning. He just might inadvertently have saved them all.

The Hopetown chamber of commerce had agreed to cosponsor the event since it would help all their businesses get a boost after the flooding they'd suffered in the fall. It would serve as notice that Hopetown had not only survived but that it was flourishing.

Abby was a PR dynamo when she got started. Ads already had been placed in the weekend section of the *Philadelphia Inquirer* for an event three weeks hence and in the local papers of municipalities all over the region, as well. She'd even secured two billboards on I-95 and was working on a Web site update. With Sam and her mother's help they'd gotten all the personal invitations to attend and stay at Cliff Walk mailed as follow-ups to the phone calls they'd made to the hotel and ski lodge general managers they'd decided to invite. The list of exhibitors Abby had compiled had been contacted already, as well.

Which left her there, alone in her room, with nothing to do but refocus on Trey and that kiss. And to dither about how she looked for a simple family dinner. Disgusted with herself, Caroline stood and stalked out her door and down the hall. If Trey could pretend that their mind-blowing kiss hadn't happened, she could, too.

Reaching desperately for calm, Caro descended the sweeping staircase as far as the shining brass chandelier that still ran on candlepower alone. That was when she caught sight of Trey's car in the drive through the two-story mullioned windows that faced the staircase. Her heart started chugging like a runaway train again.

Then Jamie entered the foyer chattering animatedly and dragging Trey by the hand. "...so that's why Mama got me the trampoline. See? Because it's good for my brain *and* fun. You can spot for me till dinner. Uncle Will used to but—" Jamie stopped, and even from where she stood Caro could see his expression grow stormy.

Trey hauled him to a stop and stepped in front of him. He sat on the dainty Louis XIV settee at the curve of the staircase. He dwarfed the piece, but she knew he'd still look right sitting on it. She peeked over the banister to look down at him. And sure enough, he did look right. Graceful. Refined. His masculinity somehow more pronounced because it stood out in sharp relief from the elegant piece.

"But what?" Trey asked, his nose still a bit above the height of Jamie's. She couldn't see Trey's expression from above but could hear concern in his voice when he went on. "Will really cares about you. Having people who love you unconditionally is a rare thing in this world. You don't throw that away because they do something you don't understand."

Why did he sound as if he knew the flip side of that sentiment? Before she could explore that troubling thought, Jamie said, "He grabbed Grandmom. And I know he kissed her even though he said it was just a hug."

Caroline was tempted to step in, but she stayed frozen in place. How much would that kiss between her and Trey have damaged Jamie's budding relationship with his father had he seen it?

"Adults kiss all the time and—" Trey began.

"I know that," Jamie interrupted, a bit of insulted pride in his snappish tone. He crossed his thin arms. "My mom told me all about that stuff about love and babies. I know my birth mom and my dad kissed and—" He stopped, then he continued with more than a bit of confusion in his tone. "Oh, but you're my dad and you and my birth mom got divorced. And that means you didn't like each other anymore."

Caroline sighed. Poor baby. So much to try to understand and all because the adults in his world had made such a tangle of things.

"I was married to your mother and I loved her. Never doubt that. But I was very busy learning how to be a doctor and she needed more time and attention than I could give her. Sometimes we can love people but not be what they need. That's how I try to think of her and our divorce."

Jamie's eyes widened. "You *knew* her! Nobody around here knew her very well. If I ask about her they don't know. Can you tell me stuff about her? I always wonder if she liked little boys."

"I guess I'm the guy to tell you then. She loved little boys. So where's this trampoline? I can tell you about her while you play on it."

They walked off, Jamie now peppering Trey with questions about Natalie's favorite foods and what his mother had smelled like. Caro sank to the step. She'd never known Jamie longed to know more about Natalie. True, he had asked her a few questions over the years, but as he'd said they had been questions she had no answers for. Should she have made up answers? No. That would have been a huge mistake, considering Trey's entrance into their lives and his intimate knowledge of Natalie.

Caro perched on the stairs as the essence of what he had said about his relationship with Natalie struck her. A feeling of grave disquiet filled the air around her. She'd never realized Trey still had been in school during his marriage to Natalie. Caro had envisioned him then as he was now, not as a young student trying to learn a difficult profession while maintaining a relationship with a woman she'd seen for herself was needy and demanding.

Sometimes we can love people but not be what they need.

Trey's version of their marriage further deviated from Natalie's depiction. And the more Caroline got to know Trey, the more she was sure he had not been any of the things Natalie had accused him of being, especially not unfaithful because that would have meant he'd given up on his marriage. The Trey she was coming to know did not strike her as the type to just walk away from a commitment like marriage. And anyway, how much spare time and energy did a med student have? Not enough to conduct the score of liaisons Natalie had accused him of having. More than likely not enough for even one.

She sighed. Another set of lives disrupted because love had warped a couple's expectations.

"Caro? Is something wrong?" her mother asked from the top of the steps.

She looked upward. "Wrong? No. Not really. I just overheard Jamie asking Trey about Natalie."

"Curiosity isn't unusual with adopted children, from what I've heard," her mother said carefully.

"Oh, no. I'm not upset about that. It's that I think maybe Natalie's version of her marriage wasn't entirely truthful. It may even have been entirely *un*truthful." And Caroline had instinctively misjudged him. What was that about? She was beginning to fear it had less to do with Jamie than she'd thought.

"Hmm. I wondered how long it would take you to begin to see Natalie's lies for what they were." Her mother had always been able to size people up quickly. Everyone but her own husband—love's bedazzling legacy again.

Shaking off that thought as unproductive, Caroline admitted, "I'm not sure she lied either. Not exactly. I think Natalie believed every word, which made her all the more convincing. Trey told Sam and Abby that Natalie was disturbed. He called her 'twisted,' but he was very kind about her just now to Jamie."

"He seems to have good instincts where Jamie's

concerned, especially now that he understands SID better, doesn't he?"

That was something else about Trey that gave Caroline pause. "It's almost uncanny. I think you were right. Trey will be good for Jamie. Could you ride herd on Sam at dinner? She's starting to calm down a little about Trey but…"

Her mother sighed. "Is she still giving him trouble?"

Caroline remembered watching Trey walking toward the cliffs yesterday while Jamie was at school. He'd rounded the corner of an equipment shed and changed directions when he'd seen Sam headed his way. "I'm not sure. I think he hides from her. This mess with Jamie wasn't his fault, even the custody-suit part of it. Not really. If I'd been more reasonable, I don't think he'd have done that."

"What mother is reasonable when faced with losing her child, Caro? Don't beat yourself up so much and don't worry about dinner. I'll handle Sammy." Juliana kicked out her high-heeled shoe for Caroline's inspection and grinned. "One of these pressing down on her little toe ought to stifle her killer instincts."

Caroline laughed at her mother's antics and stood to follow Trey and Jamie out to the trampoline. When she saw them, her heart felt as if it grew two sizes. Trey wasn't spotting for Jamie from the side of the trampoline. Instead they held hands and bounced together. Both of them seemed to be having the time of their lives. She never would have thought the man who'd come there to claim his son nearly two months ago would clown around on a trampoline like a boy.

The setting sun burnished his golden hair with copper highlights and the exertion colored his cheekbones with a healthy glow. And his lighthearted smile made her heart turn over.

"I thought the idea was to have you spot for him," she asked as she drew closer. "That's traditionally done from the ground."

Her voice startled Trey enough to break his concentration. His knees collapsed to the canvas, bringing both him and Jamie to a fumbling, bouncing halt. They both laughed as he gracefully rolled to the edge, cradling Jamie to his chest, and jumped to the ground in front of her. Even though he was clowning with Jamie, he looked a little unsettled. Did that mean the kiss had meant something to him? Or was he just worried that it meant more to her than it did to him?

"Is it dinnertime?" Jamie asked, ending the long pause in conversation.

"No, I…" She trailed off when the cell phone clipped to Trey's belt rang.

He set Jamie down and reached for it. "Dammit," he muttered as he stared at the display.

"Uh-oh. You owe the piggy a quarter," Jamie told him.

Trey shot her a pained look but showed Jamie only an embarrassed grin. Caroline was nearly sure that grin was only for Jamie's sake, because deep in Trey's eyes the troubled look remained. He stuck his hand in his pocket and handed over a quarter to Jamie. All the while the phone continued to ring. "Suppose you go pay the piggy for me," Trey suggested.

"Okay. Can I tell Grandmom what you said?" Jamie called over his shoulder.

"I wouldn't, buddy," Trey called after him.

"Not without losing a quarter of your allowance to the piggy, too," Caro declared at the same time. She and Trey looked at each other and laughed, but each sound carried a note of unease. Had one kiss destroyed all the rapport they'd developed?

The phone had gone silent but started to ring again and drew both their attention. "Aren't you going to answer that?" she asked, pointing to the phone.

Trey groaned. "I suppose I'll have to. I'm warning you, though. It isn't going to be good."

To give him some privacy Caroline turned away to watch Jamie tear through the kitchen doorway, but there was no way she could help overhearing his end of the conversation.

"Hello," he said, then his eyebrows drew together. "I see. Oh, I'm so sorry, Gordon. No, I understand completely. Really. Of course you belong at your father's side. Go. I'll work something else out."

"Problems?" she asked and turned as Trey pressed the off button on his phone.

He raked his hand through his hair and leaned against the trampoline. "That was Gordon Severs, my substitute for this week. His father had a massive heart attack in Seattle."

Caroline could see he was upset. "Is he a close friend?"

"I've known Gordon since med school. I feel bad for him, but I'm also upset about Jamie."

"You told him you'd find someone else to fill in for you. Can't you?"

Trey shook his head and winced. "I doubt it. I've

called in every favor and promised a few of my own to get here. I just started to really connect with Jamie, but I don't see any way around going home for the week. Dammit all. I hate to leave now."

"You're leaving?" Jamie cried. It was a measure of how upset he was that he didn't charge Trey another quarter fine for his language. And if that wasn't enough, the crestfallen look on Jamie's face told its own story.

Trey looked at her for help, but she had none to offer. This was something in life Jamie would have to get accustomed to. Trey didn't live at Cliff Walk. He would have to leave Jamie behind quite often, and Jamie would have to leave him after his New York visits. She knew it was early days in their relationship for him to have to learn those harsh realities, but they were realities.

"It isn't that I want to, buddy," Trey said, going down on his haunches in front of Jamie. "I have to go home to go back to my job. Someday soon, when we know each other better, you'll come to visit me where I live on weekends all the time. I'm pretty sure I'll be back next Saturday. As long as the surgeon who promised to fill in for me next week can still take my place, that is. I help fix people who get hurt in accidents. Without me or a surgeon like me, they might die. I have to go, sport."

Jamie's bottom lip quivered and his eyes filled with tears. It was encouraging that their relationship had progressed so quickly, but she hated to see her child so unhappy. Trey looked as if he were going to be the next one crying when he looked up at her. "Is there any way you two could come along? Could Jamie miss a week of school? Could you get away from the arts festival you guys are planning? I know this is bad timing but…" He trailed off and looked back at Jamie.

They both looked pitiful. Caro sighed. So now she had two irresistible males in her life. She hated to leave her mother and sisters with the festival, but the truth was there wasn't much more she could do till the weekend of the affair. Any phone calls she had left to make could be made from New York and the rest was up to her mother and Abby. The question was, did she want to venture into Trey's world when she was feeling so vulnerable to him? Then she saw that their crestfallen expressions had been replaced with ones full of hope.

What else could she do? "Oh, okay. I'm sure the others can hold down the fort here. Jamie, do you want to go see where your father lives? It's a very different place from Hopetown. It can be very noisy and busy," she warned.

Though Jamie looked instantly worried, she saw determination overshadow his automatic response almost immediately. "I want to go, Mama. I don't want him to go away from me."

She glanced toward Trey and saw something hot intensify his expression before he blinked and the look cleared away as if she'd imagined it. Had it been desire? Or a trick of the lighting. *Well, you've done it now. Whatever he'd been thinking, you've promised Jamie.* Too late to change her mind and more than a little afraid herself—though for vastly different reasons—Caroline forced herself to smile. "Then we'll go. When do you have to be back?" she asked Trey.

"It's a rare day that I'm not in surgery by six in the

morning, so I should get on the road as soon as possible. I guess I could give you directions and you could come up on your own. Do you think you could drive in New York City?"

Honestly did he think she was some country bumpkin? She crossed her arms and raised her chin. "Contrary to a typical New Yorker's opinion, Philadelphia is a rather large city with its fair share of traffic, gridlock and busy highways. If I remember correctly, parking is a huge problem in Manhattan, though. Other than that, I think I could handle anything New York could throw at me."

When Trey stood and towered over her, his eyes glittering once again, she managed not to add, *Anything but you*. Then he dropped his gaze to his watch. "Then you want to come along with me?"

Way too late now to change your mind. She clasped her hands tightly behind her back. "I suppose so. I can't chance public transportation," she added and dropped her glance down toward Jamie. As her sister had pointed out during the custody hearing, Jamie and hustle and bustle could be an explosive mix. Unfortunately Caroline was beginning to think she and Trey could be just as explosive in a whole different way. At this point she wasn't sure which was worse, but she was very afraid a week living together would answer that troubling question.

"Okay then." Trey clapped his hands. "How soon can you guys be ready?" he asked matter-of-factly in an annoyingly calm voice. Which was a good thing, she reminded herself. Still, she fought the desire to swear at him for that bloody control he always seemed to be able to conjure up whenever he needed it.

With a teeth-gritting smile plastered on her face she said, "I think we'd all better eat first."

"Oops!" Jamie squeaked. "Ms. Hannah said dinner's ready."

The tension drained out of Caroline when she saw Jamie's comical expression. Both she and Trey chuckled and turned toward the house. And all the way inside she found herself trying to dispel the deep feeling of connection she felt flowing between them. It was a bond that said *family*.

Which wasn't all that was foolish.

Both she and Trey had sworn off relationships and therefore marriage. This attraction could go nowhere. The three of them would never be a family.

She wished that didn't make her so sad.

Chapter Nine

Dinner at the manor had turned out to be a hurried affair. Which was a good thing because there was an undercurrent of mistrust coming from Samantha that made everyone uncomfortable. Trey had heard her arguing with Caroline when he'd returned to pick her up for the trip to New York.

The old adage about eavesdroppers never hearing good about themselves had certainly held true in this case. Samantha apparently thought he'd arranged the phone call so he wouldn't have to spend the entire three weeks at Cliff Walk. He even overheard her insinuate that he intended to lure Caroline and Jamie to his home turf, then refuse to let Jamie leave.

Trey wanted to be outraged, but he always tried to look at everything from two sides. To put his emotions aside and think before acting. The only times he'd let his emotions overshadow his head, he'd made huge mistakes. He'd married Natalie because she'd seemed to need him. Now he knew that he'd been so used to his mother needing him to fulfill her life that he'd mistaken need for love in Natalie's case. He'd done the same thing when he'd learned of Jamie. He'd regret that custody suit he'd filed till the day he died. He couldn't get out of his mind the image of fear in Caroline's beautiful emerald eyes as they'd sat in that courtroom. The knowledge that he'd put that fear there would haunt him for the rest of his life. Caroline, he had to admit, was a real test of his habitual iron control.

Jamie continued to be excited and animated in the car until he fell asleep, but Trey knew that wouldn't mean a thing when he had to confront the bustling city. And they were fast approaching the lights and the towering spires of New York City. Trey hoped his home would feel like an island of tranquility in the ever-flowing sea of humanity and soaring concrete structures. But as he thought about his serene, modern apartment, his worry doubled. Trey cleared his throat. "About my apartment," he began. "It's not what you and Jamie are used to."

Caroline chuckled, and the low, sexy sound shot a bolt of white-hot heat through him that went straight to his lap. And another worry clamored to the forefront of his thoughts. They'd be sharing his apartment. Sleeping across the hall from each other. This togetherness was supposed to be about him getting to know Jamie, not Caroline.

"I'm sure it will be different." Her quiet voice only

added to the hushed intimacy of the darkened car. And suddenly all he could envision was her hair spread across his tumbled bed. And what was maddening as hell was that he was sure her whispered tone was only to keep Jamie sleeping contentedly.

"How?" he asked, foolishly wanting her to keep talking.

"Well, we're used to Hopewell Manor on the banks of a quiet river. I didn't mean for you to worry this much. We'll work together and Jamie will be fine."

He remembered he hadn't told her about Mrs. Ferry. "I'm sure you'll both like my housekeeper, Mrs. Ferry. She's a gem."

"You have a housekeeper?" she asked. She sounded relieved. Was she worried about being alone with him, too?

"Mrs. Ferry's worked for me for five years. I met her in the waiting room of Mt. Sinai. Her husband, son and grandson had been in an auto accident. I was able to save Donny, her grandson, but both Mrs. Ferry's husband and her son were pronounced dead at the scene."

"How tragic."

He nodded. He'd felt so bad for the family. "By chance I stopped to visit Donny the next day and heard Mrs. Ferry telling him to stop worrying about having to move. She promised him that she planned to get a job and help his mother keep their home. As I said, I felt just terrible for her. I was also sick of fast food and doing my own laundry, so I asked her if she wanted a job with me as a live-in housekeeper and cook. She spends two days a week with her daughter-in-law and grandson in Queens. She plans to retire in a few years and live with them. She's a godsend. I know she'll get on fine with Jamie."

Close to home now, Trey checked his rearview mirror and called back to Jamie so he'd be awake and wouldn't be unprepared when they pulled up in front of the building. Sleepy-eyed, Jamie sat up and started rocking. Trey felt the now-familiar guilt sneak in to haunt him. No matter what his father said, he knew whose fault Jamie's problems were.

Five minutes later, still keyed-up over Caroline and guilt-ridden over Jamie, Trey guided the car around the corner onto Fifth Avenue and pulled up in front of his building. The Fairmont was a gem from the twenties art deco period. It had interesting lines, a magnificent tile-work facade and great views. And most important, it was a short walk from Mt. Sinai. Across from Central Park, the building was close to the reservoir where he jogged every chance he got. Unfortunately he didn't get nearly enough chances. At the end of the day it was all he could do to fall into bed.

Harry, the night doorman, appeared immediately. He unlocked the elegant glass-and-brass front doors and hurried to the car. The amiable man had Caroline's door open before Trey even had the emergency brake engaged or the trunk lock popped.

Trey hopped out and walked around the hood to hand Harry the valet key. "This is my son's mother. And this," he said as he opened the back door, "is my son, Jamie. Jamie, this is our night doorman, Mr. Washington."

Jamie stumbled out of the car, dragging his bag with him.

Harry, a man in his fifties with a wide smile and deep mahogany skin, bent down to take Jamie's bag. Jamie shrank away and Harry quickly backed off, but he looked hurt. Trey felt terrible about it. He'd thought to call ahead to warn Mrs. Ferry that guests were coming and to explain a bit about Jamie, but he hadn't thought of Harry.

Trey signaled to Caroline. "Suppose you and Jamie get in out of the chilly air and Harry and I will handle the rest of the bags. There's a whole lobby to explore, buddy, and places to sit," he added for Caroline's benefit.

A quick explanation of Jamie's problems seemed to put Harry at ease, so Trey was able to join them in the lobby moments later with the other two bags. All seemed to be going fine as Jamie walked around quietly gazing up at the paintings and examining the gilt moldings that ran around the perimeter of the lobby. He seemed fascinated with the sleek feel of it.

The elevator ride to the top of the building was a little unnerving for Jamie, but they soon exited onto the top floor. Trey's apartment was one of two penthouse apartments in the building. His was on the park side and took up two stories. The place had cost him his entire inheritance from his maternal grandfather, but it had seemed so perfect for him that he hadn't hesitated when he'd heard it was available.

He'd always thought it had a light, airy feel. The public rooms on the main floor were all open to each other and had two walls of windows that opened onto a rooftop terrace and garden. Now, though, as he opened the door and looked around, Trey instantly missed the warmth of Cliff Walk and was faintly horrified at how sterile his decor seemed. Tranquil sophistication suddenly translated to cold in the light of Caroline and Jamie's visit.

The walls were a metallic steel-gray with a wide stripe of pearly white railroaded around the room halfway between the floor and ceiling. The wall straight across from the front door and the one to the right were hung in floor-to-ceiling gray silk draperies embroidered in a diamond pattern with the occasional pearl his decorator declared would add depth. Why window coverings needed depth was still a mystery to him, but he'd written the check just the same.

Trey glanced toward the graceful open stairway that led to the bedrooms below and saw it as the safety hazard it was. The rooftop garden, with its planter-box railing, looked more like a death trap for a curious boy who could easily climb on it. Worse, the doors leading to the patio literally would be child's play to open.

As Jamie set his bag down, he bumped the console table in the foyer area. Trey's prized Dale Chihuly glass art piece wobbled. Trey held his breath but swore if it fell and wound up in a million pieces he'd laugh it off for Jamie's sake. Luckily it settled.

Then he realized that even the tables were a danger, with the sharp edges of their glass-and-steel surfaces. He pictured Jamie tripping and splitting his head open on one of the corners.

"It's…all so beautiful," Caroline said. He heard the worry in her voice, which was natural considering the near miss with the glass cylinder, but Trey knew it was more.

"Be honest. It's completely inappropriate for a boy of Jamie's age," he said, sure he was only voicing what was in her head. "I only just realized. Maybe we could rearrange things a little. I can push the sofa over in front of the stairwell."

"The stairwell could pose a problem," she admitted. "We could also put the more valuable pieces out of harm's way."

"Doctor? Is that you?" his longtime housekeeper called from the laundry room before he could tell Caroline that he didn't care about things, only people. His mother had cared about broken vases too much for that to ever be a problem for him.

"We're here, Mrs. Ferry. Come meet Jamie and Caroline," Trey called back, vowing to clear up any miscommunication with Caroline later.

Out rushed his gem of a housekeeper—all five feet two inches and one hundred seventy pounds of her. She clasped hands with Caroline. "I'm so pleased to meet you." Then she looked at Jamie and smiled broadly. "Both of you. Dr. Westerly told me all about you both. Jamie, I have your room all ready for you." That was good news. Trey had arranged to have some childhood furniture that he had in storage brought over to the apartment and he was glad to hear it had arrived.

Jamie gazed at her round face as if fascinated. "You're Mrs. Ferry? My dad told me about you, too."

"That I am. I have milk and cookies all set for you in the kitchen."

"What kind?"

"Come see."

"I'll take the bag, buddy," Trey said. Without another

word, Jamie dropped his suitcase and followed Mrs. Ferry as if mesmerized.

"When did you tell Jamie about your housekeeper?" Caroline asked as she watched Mrs. Ferry settle Jamie on a high stool at the kitchen island. Remembering her argument with Samantha, Trey understood the suspicion in her tone, but he hated it just the same.

"I wasn't preparing Jamie prematurely to come here, if that's what you're thinking. After Jamie introduced me to your housekeeper. I thought if he knew I had someone in my life like Hannah Canton, we'd have one more thing in common."

She huffed out a breath. "I'm sorry. I guess I'm nervous."

"I think it's more like your sister got to you even though you didn't want to listen to her."

"You heard," she said on a long sigh.

"Look, I swear this wasn't contrived. Gordon did have to go to Seattle to be with his father."

"I know. And I am sorry." She reached out and put her hand on his forearm. "Really. I should never have listened with even half an ear to Sam."

He didn't know how else to say it. "Natalie lied about me. I only hope you all can see that eventually."

"I already do. Believe me. Sam is bitter and angry at our father. For some reason he was always very hard on her. Then, when he didn't live up to his own impossible standards, it all but destroyed her. She's never gotten past it."

Though he didn't think any of them had gotten past James Hopewell's betrayal of their family, Trey didn't say so. Instead he motioned toward the stairwell. "Suppose we get you and Jamie settled while Mrs. Ferry has him occupied. We can talk later."

After she was sure Jamie was asleep, Caroline returned to the top floor to seek out Trey. The bedrooms were furnished with the same attention to detail as the upper floor, with the exception of Jamie's room. That was the smaller room of the three and was furnished with a well-used bedroom set that warmed up the cool tones of the walls. As he'd tucked him in, Trey had told Jamie it had been his own and that he'd had it sent there when he'd learned Jamie would come visit sometimes.

Once upstairs, Caroline noticed that Trey had already moved the sofa to block off the long side of the stairway, and the console table Jamie had knocked into now blocked its width. The glass piece that had almost taken a tumble was gone. The rearrangement threw off the symmetry of the room, but it was a good solution to an open hole in the floor that had been surrounded only with stainless-steel poles and thin, stainless chain.

Caroline took a deep breath and looked around. His apartment had shaken her. It was the home of a cosmopolitan single man with expensive taste, a big bank account and a sophisticated lifestyle. She'd begun to see him as just a hardworking doctor whose wife hadn't understood how demanding his schooling would be when they married. Caroline tried to come up with a compliment to have ready when she saw Trey because he'd seemed upset when they'd parted.

The trouble was, it looked like a museum. Perfectly put together but as cold and rigid as Trey had been when he'd arrived that first day to announce he was Jamie's father.

Chewing on her thumbnail, Caroline surveyed the apartment again. So which man was he? The caring doctor and father or the stiff, controlled automaton she'd first met?

Deciding she'd never figure it out if she avoided the talk he'd requested earlier, Caroline followed Mrs. Ferry's directions to the rooftop garden. She found Trey gazing pensively out over Central Park. "It's a lovely view," she said quietly.

A police car screamed by far below, its siren wailing. "And *so* serene," he said sarcastically.

She chuckled, hoping to keep it light. "I've heard complaints from city dwellers who stay at Cliff Walk about being kept awake by the ruckus the tree frogs and crickets kick up."

He turned, his expression grim. "But the reason behind the noise is so much different. You don't have to make me feel better about it. I know this is no place for a kid—especially one with Jamie's problems."

"I'm sure there are any number of children living in Manhattan. Some with Jamie's problems. Are you sorry we came?"

His eyes widened and showed genuine surprise. "Of course not." He gestured to a grouping of graceful chrome chairs and took her arm. She somehow managed not to shiver at the contact and thought she deserved an award since he didn't seem to notice how his touch affected her.

"I tried to warn you about the apartment when we were in the car. How could I have signed off on that decor without seeing the plans?" he asked as he took the seat across from her. "And I liked it until now. I thought it was restful."

Caroline had no answer and shrugged.

"It's Jamie. A kid sure changes your outlook on life."

Thinking about those hectic, fraught days after she'd taken Jamie on full-time, Caroline couldn't agree more. But she still had no idea what she'd missed about his not having seen plans for his apartment. "Absolutely. He certainly changed mine. At least there's Mrs. Ferry to help keep him out of trouble." He nodded and seemed to relax a bit. "She seems very nice. And talk about fast friends. She and Jamie got along wonderfully."

"Mrs. Ferry's good with kids."

Did he date women with children? Or have a lot of married friends? Caroline reined in her thoughts. How he knew about Ester Ferry and her rapport with children was none of her business. Purposely she moved on to a less personal topic. "I noticed you moved the sofa. I'm sorry if it throws off the balance of the room."

"Jamie has to be safe here," he said, his voice a bit tight.

Though he didn't say it, it must bother him that Jamie was causing so much upheaval in his life. Then she remembered that he'd also moved the glass art, so she ventured ahead. If a priceless lamp got ruined, he'd be more annoyed than he was now. "Maybe we should put away some of the more valuable pieces."

He sighed. "I moved the cylinder out of the foyer and into my room, but only because if it fell it would shatter on the marble and Jamie might get hurt."

She stared at him. He was so frustrating! "Why

won't you stay in your box?" she demanded without thinking, then couldn't think of anything to say when he raised an eyebrow and grinned, silently daring her to explain. Pride forced her to do just that. "This apartment doesn't fit the man who made sure Jamie had a new swing or who bounced on the trampoline earlier tonight or who took such pleasure from a simple picnic last week. So I got here and readjusted my conception of you back to the controlled, sophisticated New Yorker I first met. Now you're not him again. Why are you more annoyed that the apartment is wrong for Jamie than that Jamie is wrong for the apartment?"

Trey's challenging gaze had become intent, Caroline noticed. She felt like a lab experiment pinned to a Petri dish.

"What box are you talking about?" he asked, his eyes narrow and determined.

Had she actually blurted all that out? What was wrong with her? He was what was wrong, darn it all!

"I don't know who you are," she fired back. "You keep changing type. I need to know who my son's father is and I can't figure you out. Good Lord!" She pinched the bridge of her nose. "I'm starting to wonder who in the wide, green world *I* am at this point."

"Ah." He grinned slyly again, as if he'd had a sudden revelation, and her stomach bounced a second time. "You like to size people up and you expect them to act accordingly," he went on. The man was so annoyingly right she found herself grinding her teeth. "First your banker flips from family friend to enemy and now I guess I've done it to you, too. When we met, you had a preconceived notion of me, thanks to Natalie. And I played right into it."

He leaned forward. "Who am I? Truthfully, Caroline, I've come closer to answering that question since meeting you and Jamie than I ever have. The sad thing is I don't think I'd ever even considered the question until you both came along. You challenged me to examine my life because of how you live yours. The best I can do at this point is tell you who I'm not. I'm not the nightmare husband Natalie apparently pegged me as. I'm not even the man who took you to court. And I'm sure not that apartment in there. Not anymore, at least." He paused, frowning. "If I ever was.

"The only thing I bought after I bought this place was that Chihuly glass art. My mother recommended a decorator and the two of them handled it for me. Mrs. Ferry and I showed up and moved in bag and baggage after it was ready. And Mother and her decorator were horrified by the Chihuly. It's all wrong for the space, apparently—whatever the hell that means."

"Why did you hire a decorator who didn't understand you?"

"Long story. Mother recommended her as a lot more than a decorator. She thought we were perfect for each other. I was trying to appease both of them by hiring the woman. Look at how she decorated my home." He raked his hand through his hair. "Sadder yet, I didn't realize how much it isn't me until I thought of walking in with you and Jamie."

"I'm surprised you gave that much control to someone else."

"Natalie again?" he asked, then pressed his lips into a tight line. He stood and walked to the planter boxes, once again looking out over Central Park. "I'm not a control freak. Yes, I did try to get Nat to take control of her emotions. I just wanted her to stop causing scenes. I'll even admit I try to control my own emotions. If I didn't, I'd have taken a dive off this roof long ago over all the patients I've lost. I lose more than most surgeons because I'm trying to fix damage, not illness. A bullet or a jagged piece of metal or a sixty-mile-an-hour crash are more indiscriminate. I have a harder and less precise job than a skilled surgeon with a scalpel seeking out disease."

She followed him for reasons she couldn't fathom. Maybe it was the pain in his voice over all the strangers his talent hadn't been enough to save. Maybe it was the stiffness with which he held himself. She nearly laughed at the irony. Did he really believe he had his emotions in check? She could easily disabuse him of that notion by pointing out the slight quaver in his voice when he talked of losing patients. Or she could remind him of the times he'd been affected by something Jamie said or did. Maybe it was that Jamie had changed him more than he realized. But if that was the case, he'd given up a lot of his prized control already. Caro didn't think it wise to push him further or to mention it, lest he guard himself too closely.

"What about you?" he challenged, turning to glare down at her. "You and your boxes. Do you even know you live in one yourself?" His eyes looked like twin lasers.

And they burned her, setting off an angry passion she'd never felt before. "Do I?" she asked, standing a bit straighter, refusing to show how much she wanted him to lose some of that control of his because of her.

"You've given your entire life to raising someone else's child, taking care of your family and building that vineyard, but you don't have anything else. From the outside it looks like your life is full, but what about you? What about the woman inside you? Jamie's going to grow up one day and go off on his own. Your sisters may actually find a way to trust a man with their hearts and build lives of their own. If Will has his way, your mother sure will. What will you have then?"

"I like the life I built. It was what it was—at least until you came along and stirred it up."

She had no real warning but the sizzle in the air between them. He reached out and grabbed her hips, pulling her against him, leaving little doubt that she aroused him, too. She tried to back away but he held fast.

"Did I stir up your life? Do I stir you as much as you do me?" he demanded. "Are you going to deny this part of you for the rest of your life?" He bent his head then, taking her lips in a kiss that set off explosions inside of her.

Of their own accord, her arms circled his neck and she held on for dear life. Why she trusted him to keep her safe from the tumult battering her she didn't know.

If the air had sizzled moments ago, it caught fire now as his tongue sought hers. And with the deepening of the physical connection between them he spun out of control. Trey dropped back onto the edge of the big cement planter box and widened his stance to pull her tightly against his burgeoning arousal.

Caroline heard a raw sound of need escape her own throat, and it called her back to sanity. She dropped her hands to his shoulders and pressed.

Trey lifted his head, staring down at her, his gaze burning into hers. She felt a tremor rock his body. "Why?" he asked, his voice whiskey-rough.

"Because this isn't smart and it can't go anywhere that wouldn't make the rest of our lives more complicated and uncomfortable."

He tightened the hands that still held her hips. "I'm pretty damned uncomfortable right now. I meant, why *you?* Why do you make me feel this way?" His eyes were as bright as twin flames. And he was still annoyed. Or annoyed again.

She didn't know how she felt about him having the nerve to be irritated after kissing her. Did he think he was the only one uncomfortable? The only one that kiss had set on fire with no hope of having the flames extinguished? *He* had kissed *her*. How dare he blame her for how that kiss had made him feel. "What way do I make you feel? Say it," she baited him.

"Out of control. Okay? Is that what you wanted to hear? I want the hell out of you. And I don't know what to do about it. What's worse, since halfway through that ill-conceived court hearing, I've cared about you. If I didn't, I'd haul you downstairs and get this over with. But you aren't just some bed partner I can enjoy and wave goodbye to. You're my son's mother."

Now Caroline did push out of his arms. She stepped back and brushed the hair out of her eyes. "And you're stuck with me? Is that it? Well, pal," she said and poked his muscular chest, "I'm just as stuck with you. I swore off feeling all these messy emotions years ago. And for the record—no one hauls me into bed unless I want to be there. No one has even tempted me in years, least of all you."

"Are you afraid of sex?" he goaded.

Her cheeks grew warm but not through embarrassment. She was good and angry now. "I will not have sex for mere physical release. I don't think I can be involved in something that intimate and not have my feelings moved. And I will never trust love again."

"Why?"

"It changes people from perfectly reasonable and trustworthy to strangers even to themselves."

Trey's eyes narrowed and he studied her for a long, uncomfortable moment. "This can't be over what your father did. Who was he?"

"He who?" she stalled.

"The one who hurt you so bad you hide from your womanhood."

Fine. He wanted to know. She'd tell him. "I was engaged when Mama caught my father at a party with his intern. Kyle was appalled. He didn't like his name attached to a scandal. I'd given him everything and he walked away without looking back. I wish I could say he didn't hurt me, but he did. And worse, I felt stupid—and I'm never going to feel stupid again. So do us both a favor and keep your hands to yourself!"

She whirled away and stalked toward the doors to the apartment and heard him mutter, "I wish it were that easy."

Well, I do, too! Caroline mentally paid the fine jar, then went ahead with the thought. *I do, too, dammit!*

Chapter Ten

Trey stepped inside the foyer of his home two nights later. He hadn't seen Caroline—or Jamie, for that matter—since Monday night. The place was quiet, with only the subdued sound of Mrs. Ferry's TV humming in the background. Though a cowardly part of him that hated confrontation longed to put off talking to Caroline, he knew he couldn't any longer. Not after picking up his messages.

He'd made a strategic error earlier in the day when he'd forwarded his cell phone calls to his office the way he usually did. When Trey's secretary answered, his mother knew he'd returned to New York and that Jamie and Caroline were with him. He'd spoken to her just before leaving his office to prep for surgery and told her not to contact them—that New York was too upsetting for Jamie and that he'd see that they got together to-morrow.

But of course his mother hadn't listened. She'd left a message on his voice mail and she hadn't painted a pretty picture of the day. It had brought back painful memories of scenes with her from his childhood.

Apparently she had swept down on Caroline and Jamie like an avenging fury. It didn't help that she'd brought her evil little dog along. Then Mrs. Ferry left a message telling him just about the same thing but, of course, with a slant that didn't show his mother as the victim of the piece. Because he'd been in the middle of a futile seven-hour surgery, he'd missed both messages until a few minutes ago. He was also afraid it was very telling that there'd been no message from Caroline.

Tired and disheartened after losing a thirty-year-old father of five, Trey tossed his jacket over one of the club chairs near the fireplace and stopped, seeking the serenity he always found in the quiet colors and calm lines. Something, he realized, was missing. He noticed the video learning system he'd had his secretary order for Jamie to make up for his absence last night. It lay on the floor in front of the entertainment center. Jamie had obviously played with it.

His gaze moved upward from the floor to the top of the TV unit. Trey had sent Caroline flowers and a note of apology for his unforgivable behavior on the terrace. They were sitting on top of the sleek armoire that housed his television gear and stereo. At least she hadn't thrown the flowers in the trash, he thought grimly.

There was a light out on the terrace, so Trey forgot about the feeling that something was absent and followed the light across the dimly lit living room. Caroline sat on the chaise, cradling Jamie against her side. Both of them looked as if it had been a hard day. Jamie was sound asleep with his head pillowed on Caroline's breast. Trey found it was a bit of an effort not to feel jealous of his son at that moment.

Caroline, too, was asleep. Her eyes were closed and her head had fallen back against the cushions, exposing the delicate lines of her throat. She was so beautiful it made his heart ache just to look at her. Her creamy complexion looked translucent and seemed to capture the moonlight. The need to touch that pearly skin drew his hand like a magnet.

At the touch of his fingertips, Caroline opened her eyes and stared up at him. She opened her mouth, but he laid his finger over her lips.

"Shh. I'll put him in bed, then we'll talk. Okay?"

She nodded and Trey bent to scoop Jamie gently into his arms. But his hand brushed her breast, she gasped and they both froze, staring at each other. His heart pounded and a corresponding pulse throbbed low in his body. Before that became obvious to her, he clutched Jamie close and beat a hasty retreat.

His mind and body collected, he returned minutes later and found her standing in his favorite spot overlooking the park.

"Trey, I don't know how to say this," she said and paused before pivoting toward him. "No. I do. I've come to see you as a very nice person and I don't want to insult you, but your mother is the most impossible woman I've ever met."

He sighed. *Mother, why couldn't you for once have*

done what I asked and waited to descend on them until I was here? He was so tired and tempted to just turn and walk away, but a mother of five was making funeral arrangements tonight. He didn't feel entitled to be a coward. If she could face telling those children their father would never come home, who was he to avoid dealing with the fallout from his mother?

"Mrs. Ferry left me a message. She said mother had caused all manner of problems today. Something about that mongrel masquerading as a lapdog. What did the ankle biter do?"

"The dog was a problem, yes, but he was just acting like a dog. It was more your mother's attitude. It started with the dog running. So Jamie started chasing him. One or both of them knocked into a table and broke a lamp. I'm sorry about it. I'll replace it."

That's what was missing and why the room had been so dim. Oh, well. "I don't care about a lamp. Come on over here and sit. You look ready to fall over." After they were seated across from each other he said, "So what happened next?"

"Your mother started shouting about the value of the lamp, and the dog started barking again. Jamie couldn't handle all the noise. He had a full-blown, throw-himself-on-the-floor tantrum."

"Mother really dotes on Inky," he tried to explain.

Caroline glared at him and continued her tale of woe. "I got Jamie calmed down, but your mother refused to sequester her precious *Inky* in the laundry room. So it started all over again. It was lunchtime and I got Jamie calm enough to eat, but she made a big deal because he had headphones on at the table."

"Table manners are a big thing to her. She's from a different generation than we are," he said, but he knew his defense sounded weak.

"Are you defending her?" Caroline demanded.

Trey didn't answer right away. Was he? "Yes. No! I'm just trying to explain her, I suppose. Go on. I'm sure it didn't end there."

"After lunch she insisted we take Jamie to the Guggenheim Museum. I said no, but she'd made the suggestion in front of Jamie. He's been feeling a little cooped up and wanted to go out. She pointed out a finger painting he'd done for Mrs. Ferry and told him he'd learn how to do a better one if he saw real paintings. He begged to go, but I was afraid it was going to be a disaster. So she started complaining to Mrs. Ferry that I was being inflexible. Again in front of Jamie."

He recognized the divide-and-conquer tactic his mother had used to drive a wedge between him and his father. "So how did the trip go?" he asked, knowing without asking that his mother had gotten her way and wondering what he was going to do about her.

"We got there with relative ease, really. Mrs. Ferry called for a cab and had it waiting out front, and frankly Jamie was fascinated with all the cars and trucks."

Trey knew that wouldn't have lasted once they reached the museum. He remembered his own first trip there. His mother had actually expected him to walk around there with his hands in his pockets and just look at those confusing blotches and slashes of color. He didn't imagine things had changed. After his reading on SID, Trey understood the problem caused by too much sensory input and so he now understood why he'd been unable to control his own impulses. And he knew Jamie would have had even more trouble.

The paintings at the museum were hung along the walls of a wide ramp that wound down through the center of the building, instead of separate floors connected by stairs and elevators. Trey remembered the temptation to let gravity have its way and careen heedlessly down the ramp. "Jamie wanted to run down the ramp, I imagine."

"It was a disaster. He tripped constantly. Both his knees are skinned. We stayed less than an hour. Your mother wanted to go shopping so the day wouldn't be a complete waste. I said no way and the next thing I knew, she'd left."

He flinched. He was always wincing over his mother. "Mother rarely comes to the city anymore and she's easily overwhelmed," he said weakly, hoping again to explain his mind-boggling mother.

But rather than appease Caroline, it made those green eyes of hers shoot sparks. "Which left me to try flagging down a taxi with Jamie in tow—who we both know is very easily overwhelmed! That's where the fascination with the cars ended for him. All the horns beeping and the traffic whizzing by terrified him. Then, when we finally got home, that dog was still here terrorizing Mrs. Ferry."

"I'm sorry."

She glared. "I'm not through. Marilyn returned at dinnertime on her way home to pick up the dog. She was furious to find him locked in the laundry room. Jamie so wanted her approval. He can't understand that she isn't like my mother. He showed her a new finger painting he'd done for you after we got home. He thought it was a good likeness for the paintings we'd seen today. So did I. He was so proud. Your mother looked down her nose at it and said he had far to go before he'd be in the same league as Picasso. You should have seen his face!" Caroline looked as if she was about to cry and/or shout at any moment.

"I'm sorry she was such a trial."

"It isn't your job to apologize for her. If Jamie hadn't been there, I would have told her off for hurting him."

Trey knew it wouldn't have done any good. His mother wouldn't have heard a thing Caroline said. He guessed he should have reined her in years ago. Guilt gnawed at him. "I'll handle my mother."

"You'd better or I will," she warned.

"Just give me some time," he asked, knowing what an impossible task lay before him.

"Time? Do you have any? Trey, I'm not sure I understand why we came. Jamie hasn't seen you."

"I know. And I'm sorry. That's why I sent the game over for him. I got him some more DVDs for it today."

"You said people are more important to you than things. What makes you think it's any different for Jamie?"

That gave him pause. "I don't. I felt guilty for dragging him here and getting sucked in at the hospital. I'm off rotation tomorrow." Exhausted both physically and emotionally and hoping for a few minutes of pleasant conversation, Trey tried to swing the subject into new territory, "So how was your evening? Better than the day, I hope."

* * *

Now that she'd gotten her anger out at someone who might be able to do something about it, Caroline noticed how tired and disheartened Trey looked. For the first time it occurred to her that hers may not have been the only bad day floating around New York. "Is something wrong other than getting hit with complaints about Marilyn and—" she checked her watch "—not getting home till ten when I heard you leave around five-thirty or six this morning? It was even later last night."

"I'll sleep in tomorrow. Maybe we can take Jamie into the park if it's a nice day. There are boats to rent and horses, too."

It sounded wonderful after the nightmare day she'd had, but she still wanted to hear about his day. "That's tomorrow. What about today? Are you this tired every night?"

"The day ended on a down note."

"So tell me about it. Listening is the least I can do after unloading on you practically the second you walked through the door."

He shrugged, then admitted, "I lost a patient. Thirty years old. Husband. Father of five."

"What went wrong?"

He let out a deep breath. "Too much blood loss. Too much time on the table. Not enough time to fix it all. There was a pileup on the expressway. They airlifted him but…"

"But there was too much damage. Right?" She wanted to reach out to him. Was this supposed to be evidence of that iron control he'd talked about?

"I'd stop one hemorrhage and he'd spring a leak somewhere else. We couldn't get the transfusions into him fast enough. Minutes count on the front end, too. He was trapped for half an hour. Seven hours on my table and I still lost him. I always feel like such a failure when I lose someone so young who fought so hard to live."

"At least because of you he had a chance. That's something he'd never have had in and around Hopetown."

Trey's tired gaze sharpened. "What do you mean?"

"They had to close the trauma centers at Central Bucks Memorial and St. Stephen's. The great Pennsylvania physician exodus strikes again. Now accident victims have to be airlifted into Philadelphia."

He frowned, thoughtful. "That's ridiculous with I-95 so close and all the serious accidents that happen there."

"I know, and we get a lot of heavy traffic in the area during the summer months because of Hopetown, Fairytale Village up the road and Blairsville across the river from it. Those back roads see some pretty horrific crashes, too. But still, it's a wonderful place to raise Jamie."

"You're lucky to live somewhere so magical." He yawned expansively. "Oh, I'd better turn in before I fall asleep out here again." He got up and looked down at her. "This was nice." He bent down and kissed her softly. "Thanks. As always, you're easy to talk to, and I guess I needed a friendly ear. I'll see you and Jamie in the morning."

Caroline watched him walk in the house and covered

her tingling lips with her fingers. Why did he make her feel these things? Why him? Why now?

And what on earth was she going to do about it? Trey Westerly would be so easy to love. And love was something she'd sworn to never trust again. It had failed her mother. It had failed her.

Carrying Jamie on his shoulders, Trey bounced out of the elevator and over to his door. Jamie giggled, a different boy today than he'd been yesterday. Laughing and carefree, they burst into the apartment. Trey stopped dead and she ran into his back. And came face-to-face with a nightmare.

"Mother? Dad?"

Caroline heard Trey's voice go from lighthearted to stiff in a millisecond. She drew back from Trey and looked at the picture his parents made. They looked as if a battle of sorts had gone on. Marilyn, her face in high color, sat as far across the living room area as she could without being on the rooftop terrace. Her back was stiff, her lips pinched.

His father sat at the breakfast bar as if conversing with Mrs. Ferry, looking much more relaxed, but the muscle throbbing at the side of his angular jaw told a different story. Trey's father was a good-looking man who had obviously passed his looks to his son. It was like looking at Trey years down the line.

Wes Westerly smiled nervously and walked toward them. "I had to come into the city for a consult, so I dropped by to leave some toys Rob sent along to pass on to Jamie." He gestured to a sizable stack of toys. "I don't know exactly what's appropriate, but I looked over most of it. I think there are some interesting things over there this young man might like to play with. So you're Jamie," he said with a wide smile. "It's wonderful to meet you."

He turned, after shaking Jamie's hand, toward her with his hand held out in greeting. Caroline found herself automatically reaching out to respond. He gripped her hand in both of his, his smile warm and engaging. Trey's father was obviously quite a charmer. "Call me Wes, Caroline," he said, still pressing her hand between his. "It's such a pleasure to meet you."

"Toys?" Marilyn Guilford asked, her tone as petulant as a bratty thirteen-year-old's. "Trying to bribe him the same way you did Trey?"

Trey's father let go of Caroline and glanced toward his ex-wife. After a long pause he shook his head and muttered in a stage whisper, "Reminds me why it's been twenty-five years since I sat in a room with her unless it was a courtroom."

"Say hello to your grandfather," Trey said, swinging Jamie carefully to the floor and ignoring the waspish byplay between his parents. Or trying to, Caroline decided when she saw his tight expression. She was suddenly quite grateful to both her parents for not having put her and her sisters in untenable situations like this. Trey must have grown up feeling like the rope in a tug-of-war. It had never occurred to her how much worse her parents divorce could have been.

Jamie looked up at Wes, then glanced across the room at his grandmother. "Are you married to her?" he asked, pointing across the room toward Trey's mother.

Wes grinned. "No, pal. Not any longer." Then a

"Thank the Good Lord" growl rumbled out in an undertone. "Why don't you take a look at those toys?"

Jamie tugged on her sweater, silently asking permission. His suddenly troubled look told her he felt the waves of tension coming from the adults in the room. He'd done so well today. Caroline hated having Jamie witness a scene like this—one so totally outside his experience. It could easily ruin the day for him.

"Looking at the toys is such a good idea," she said as cheerfully as she could. "Let's go see what your uncle Rob sent for you." Caroline held out her hand and led Jamie over to the pile of toys. "See these, Jamie." She picked up the cardboard drum and rattled it. "I've seen these before. They're called Lincoln Logs. Let's go over to the breakfast bar and see if we can build a log cabin like the one in the picture."

Mrs. Ferry, bless her, was already bustling around in the kitchen. "Lincoln Logs! Oh, I just love those! Could I get in on this building project, Jamie? If I give you milk and cookies, may I play, too?"

Jamie's frown as he dumped the barrel on the counter was thankfully more one of concentration than worry. "Sure. I don't know how to build with these. They aren't square."

Mrs. Ferry sent her a look that said shoo and took over. Hoping to defuse an upsetting scene, Caroline returned to Trey's side.

"Griff's coming in this weekend," she heard his father say as she approached them. "Danielle's planning a big family weekend. We even had the pool opened in case the weather's warm enough to swim." He clapped Trey on the arm. "Bring Jamie and Caroline up to the house. The kids are dying to meet him. We'll all be disappointed if you guys can't be there."

Marilyn stormed across the room. "Oh, no you don't. Trey knows I have a charity picnic for Mt. Sinai planned for Saturday. And there's a kickoff cocktail party for it tomorrow night. It's always the fourth Friday of May."

Trey was back on rotation tomorrow, and when he reminded his mother of that, she still expected him to put in a late appearance. No thought seemed to be given to how tired he'd be by that time or that Jamie wouldn't have seen him all day.

"But I—" Trey began, but Wes stepped on his words.

"When are you going to stop monopolizing all his free time?" Wes demanded of his ex-wife.

"I'd rather just—" Trey started again, but this time his mother broke in.

"This is to benefit his hospital! And I do not monopolize his time. Do I, son?"

"Well you—" he tried, but his father was quicker.

"Have you ever asked him if he has other plans? I can't tell you how many times Danielle and I have invited him up but he already had plans you'd never let him out of. You drag him out when he should be catching up on his sleep. My kids want to meet their nephew. And you spent the day with Jamie already. According to Mrs. Ferry, you also upset him. It's our turn to have him with us."

"I was the one who raised Trey. His son should get to know me first."

If Caroline felt like a spectator at a tennis match, then Trey must be feeling like the ball. She wasn't having this for Jamie. "We'll be headed back to Hopetown by then," she broke in, hoping to stop the nasty byplay. Maybe if they realized how much Trey had on his plate already they'd both back down. "And please keep your voices down, both of you. Jamie has had a good day and I won't have this upsetting him."

Wes colored, touched his forehead and after a pause said, "I'm so sorry." He shook his head sadly. "Five minutes and we're back at it. Trey, you do what you think is best, but we would all love to have you come up. It would be a great weekend." He checked his watch. "I'd better get to my meeting. If you'll excuse me, I'll just say goodbye to Jamie."

"Well, that certainly wasn't an unexpected pleasure," Marilyn sneered. "Honestly, Trey, I don't know why you continue to encourage that man to insinuate himself in your life. Now that he's gone, we should be making plans for this weekend. Caroline, what a shame you have to go home on Friday."

Marilyn turned in such a way as to exclude Caroline before she could inform the older woman that Jamie also would be in Hopetown by Friday night or at the latest Saturday morning.

Trey looked shell-shocked as he stared in clear disbelief at his mother.

"So, darling," Marilyn said, barely having taken half a breath, "what time do you think you can get to the cocktail party? And, oh, Jamie will need a suit. I suppose I can take him to get one. You'll want to introduce him to your colleagues and then he can spend the evening upstairs. I can get that little maid I just hired to watch him."

"Mother, you can't take Jamie shopping and I'd

never bring Jamie without his mother. I don't know enough yet about the things that set him off."

Marilyn gazed up at Trey's frowning countenance and sighed. "No, I suppose not. I never should have wished you'd have a child like yourself all those years ago, but now I suppose you finally understand how hard it was on me. I'll just go pick up a couple of suits for him and you can try them on him here." She bustled toward the front door. "I think blue. Wool. Yes, definitely wool," she said as the door closed behind her.

"What just happened to you?" Caroline demanded after silence reigned for a few moments. "You just agreed that we'd go to your mother's by default."

"No. I'll handle her. She just doesn't understand."

"Do that. But for the record, Jamie and I will be headed home on Friday night. If you get tied up or decide not to *handle* her, I'll call for a rental so you don't have to worry about pleasing us, too. You have some decisions to make, Trey. Decisions you should have made before you came into Jamie's life. He needs more than a fraction of a father. After work and your obligations to your parents, that's all you have left to give him."

Chapter Eleven

Trey raked a hand through his hair and watched Caroline stride over to Jamie and Mrs. Ferry at the breakfast bar. Once in the kitchen, she pasted on a ready smile for them. But when she looked back at him over their bent heads, she sent him a fulminating look.

Whoa. That was one angry woman.

How, he wondered, could he have come to know her so quickly when he'd come to know almost nothing about the women in his past even after being around them for months? Maybe, he thought, watching Caroline, it was that she had such an innate honesty that her heart was an open book.

Open now because he'd learned to look past the thin surface. Perhaps that was the difference between his relationship with her and any woman in his past, even with his late ex-wife. He wanted to see more of her, find out more.

Just as at their first meeting, right now her anger was all about her fear for Jamie. And he guessed she was right. He did have a lot to think about. But he had just as much to explain to her. Because while she had been completely honest with him, he was hiding his secret shame and therefore the fallout from it made no sense to her. If he explained what a shambles he'd made of his parents' marriage and therefore of his mother's life, Caroline would understand and be more tolerant of her. He was sure of it. She was too compassionate a person to refuse to make allowances for his mother's obsession with him.

Before he had a chance to change his mind, Trey followed her. "Caroline, could we talk? Please?"

Startled, she glanced up from her building project, a silky golden wave of her hair covering one eye. The other electric-green eye glittered with anger. "I don't think we have anything to say to one another right now."

"Yes, we do."

"Mama, that doesn't go that way," Jamie protested, then giggled, drawing both their attention to the building project in the works.

Caroline sputtered a laugh. "No. I guess not," she admitted. Obviously chagrined, she took off the long log that protruded from the half-built cabin wall like the arm of a crane.

Jamie looked up at him, wearing that heart-melting, teasing smile of his. "Mama's not very good at log cabins. Maybe could she play Chutes and Ladders or Candy Land with you, Daddy?"

Trey knew what it felt like to be hit with lightning. *Daddy*. His son had called him Daddy. That simple word, with all its major ramifications, hit him like a blow to the solar plexus. He swallowed and couldn't seem to get his breath. He blinked rapidly to clear his vision. Oh, but this kid could bring him to his knees so easily it was terrifying.

"Come along," he heard Caroline say somewhere in the recesses of his brain. Then he felt a tug on his arm, so he obeyed her urging. "Take a breath before you melt into a puddle in front of him, *Daddy*." He heard the chuckle in her voice but for the life of him he couldn't react.

With her still all but leading him, they stepped out onto the terrace. His legs felt a little wobbly, so when she pressed on his shoulders, he sank obediently into one of the chaises. Caroline snapped her fingers in front of his face and he blinked. He knew he had a goofy-looking grin on his face but couldn't seem to care. "We're on the terrace," he said inanely, trying to show her how together he was.

She rolled her eyes. "Very good. We need to talk, Trey."

"I know." He did. He really did. Talking had been his idea. He wanted to clear things up with her, but she looked so serious and he wasn't ready for serious yet. He didn't want to let go of the buoyant feelings suffusing him. "What did you want to talk about?" he asked, hoping she wasn't ready for deep subjects either.

"You shouldn't let him see you react like that, you idiot." She laughed, taking the sting out of the comment.

"I guess not."

"You guess? He'll have you wrapped around his little finger. Actually he already does," she said and smiled again. "But it would be good if he didn't know it."

Trey relaxed a little. She wasn't angry anymore. "Right. I'll work on it. I was afraid he'd be too big before he got comfortable enough with me to call me Daddy. I've missed so much. I didn't want to miss that, too. Now I won't."

Caroline continued smiling kindly as she sat in the chair across from the chaise. "I'm glad neither of you will miss it," she said. "Trey, listen to me." She leaned forward, an earnest look on her lovely face. "Jamie has problems but he isn't stupid. And he's sweet-natured but he isn't beyond playing you. All he has to do is look at something and you're offering to get it for him. A horse? You offered to buy him a horse earlier."

He just wanted Jamie to have the best he could give him. Spirit had made him so happy. "He showed me your old stables at Hopewell Manor. They could be fixed up easily. I had a horse and it did me so much good. It taught me responsibility and I used to ride constantly." He didn't add especially when his parents were fighting over him.

"Yeah. Until your mother got rid of him—and that still hurts you. I'm not sure I can afford to take on an animal that needs that much special care and feeding. I'd rather not scar my son with a loss like that if the cost gets to be too much of a burden." Her expression grew fierce. "But I can tell you this—if he had one already, I'd fight tooth and nail before I just got rid of it."

She wasn't talking about Jamie's horse. She was talking about Spirit and him. She was angry at his mother on his account. Trey was touched beyond words. Then, like smoke easing into a room to silently fill it and eat up all the light, he remembered. His mother. Jamie's problems. His own guilt attached to both. That was what he'd wanted to talk to her about before Jamie had offhandedly cut him off at the knees.

Trey closed his eyes and took a deep breath. "She got rid of Spirit because I was away at school. It was my fault I lost Spirit because it was my fault she sent me to boarding school. Everything that's gone wrong in her life is my fault. That's why I give in to her. Her life is empty except for me—because of me."

She blinked and sat straight. "Oh, don't be ridiculous. What could you possibly do—other than give in to her every whim—to make her the way she is? She's an adult."

He kneaded the tense muscles of his neck for a few seconds, trying to get up the nerve to say what had to be said. What was so hard about admitting the truth? His parents knew what he'd been like. How awful he'd been. And now he at least knew why. "Everything that's gone wrong for you with Jamie is my fault, too, Caroline. I was like Jamie is. Maybe not as impacted, but I've been seeing similarities between us since the day I tried to teach him tennis. My dad does, too. He even sees similarities to himself as a child."

"Then why on earth doesn't your mother understand him if she had a son like him?" He opened his mouth to explain, but her eyes widened, sharpened. "Oh. I get it. That was what that crack was about her wishing you'd have a child like you were. She sent you to boarding school because you were too much trouble. What a witch!"

He shook his head. "No. Because I *caused* so much trouble," he corrected. Didn't she get what he was saying? "Jamie's problems are my fault, too," he said, deliberately emphasizing each word.

Caro shrugged carelessly. "I knew he could have inherited it from someone." Then her gaze sharpened. "And you've been feeling guilty about it? Now that I think about it, you more or less asked if it was your fault that day at the tennis court, but I didn't understand that you were talking about the SID. Don't you see what good news this is? Look at how far you've gone in life. Look at your father. Once we get Jamie past all this, he's going to be just fine. More than fine." She smiled, blinking back tears. "This is like seeing a light at the end of a long, dark tunnel. It's all I've ever wanted for him."

Well, now, that gave him pause. But there was still all the fallout from those early years of his life. "But just because I'm normal now, that doesn't change all the damage I did to my parents. I was the reason for their divorce."

Her eyes sparked again. "They told you that?" she demanded, then before he could correct her, she held up her hand. "No. You don't even have to say it. *She* told you that. I reiterate. What a witch!"

"You don't understand the full scope of it. I'm the reason my mother didn't have more children with my stepfather, Earl. That's why she's so focused on me. Dad has other kids so, much as I'd rather spend more time with him, I defer to Mother if there's a conflict."

"Trey, listen to yourself." She moved to the bottom of the chaise and cupped his cheek.

Trey's brain, such as it had recovered from Jamie's little surprise, melted into a puddle of need. She seemed to be offering him the one thing he'd never had from a woman. Complete understanding and acceptance.

"She's blamed you for everything that's wrong in her life. She's made you feel guilty so you wouldn't see her as she is—selfish."

"I know she's selfish but that's because she only has herself to think about. Earl's busy all the time with his practice."

"She didn't even know your problems could be passed on genetically. Which means her only excuse for not having more children is that she was too selfish to dedicate herself to raising them properly. I heard you talking to Jamie about not throwing away unconditional love. You value it so much because she's never loved you the way anyone's child deserves. The truth is your mother couldn't deal with your problems so she stuck you in a boarding school. And that's where all this drive to control your emotions came from. That's what they taught you. It has nothing to do with your work."

Trey nodded. "I'm not doing so good with that these days," he whispered. He'd figured out that much on his own, but she'd worked out the rest. He'd never known that having someone care about his private pain could be so seductive. "I don't have any control around you," he added in the same low tone as he sat up and slid forward, nearer to her. "None at all," he added and leaned closer still, giving in to the need that her nearness, understanding and compassion had sent raging through him.

He didn't know why he couldn't be near her without wanting her any more than he understood why she was able to unlock the innermost yearnings of his heart with a kind word. All he knew at that moment was that her lips were soft as the spring breeze that eddied about the terrace. Her mouth was sweet as the ice cream she'd eaten in the park. And her hands—those perfect, incredibly soft hands—clutched at his shoulders, then slid into his hair as he pulled her with him back onto the chaise.

He traced her back, the curve of her bottom, pressing her nearer his aching arousal. Then he gloried in the sounds she couldn't hold back. Trey broke the kiss. "Come to my room tonight after Jamie's asleep. I want you so much I can't fight it anymore. I swear, if I don't have you soon, I'll lose what's left of my mind."

"We can't, Trey. Think. Oh, God, we have to think what would happen if Jamie saw us."

"You want this…you want me…as much as I want you." She opened her mouth to either protest or agree but he didn't want to talk. To hear her deny the truth. He found her lips again, letting his mouth do the persuading for him. He slipped his tongue past her lips to stroke her luxurious mouth in a bold imitation of his heart's desire. Luring her. Tempting her. Daring her to pretend she didn't want to go the same place he did.

The mood turned magic. He'd just found her peaked nipple when behind his back Jamie's voice shattered the enchanted moment. "Mrs. Ferry said dinner's—oh! I'll tell Mrs. Ferry you don't want dinner." A few scuffing sounds followed and Trey held his breath. From farther away, in the rush of what sounded like one breath, Jamie continued, "Mama? Daddy? Can I get a baby sister instead of a brother like Matthew? Matthew has to share his room with his baby brother, and I want to still be able to play in my room in the afternoon when he comes over." Inside the house a split second later he shouted, "Mrs. Ferry! They're making a baby so now…"

Trey lifted his head and stared at Caroline's horrified expression. His lips twitched and he felt something break inside. Laughter bubbled up from the depths of his soul. Even when her expression went from horrified to supremely annoyed, then somewhere past that, he couldn't stop laughing. Tears poured down his cheeks and she swatted his shoulder before scooting to the end of the chaise.

"Stop it," she demanded, jumping to her feet, her cheeks flaming. "How can you laugh? We may have just scarred our son."

"Oh, he sounded real scarred. What was it you said? I try to give him everything he asks for? I'd be more than…" He started howling again at her look of outrage. Unfortunately even the idea of what it would take to give Jamie his every wish in this instance added to Trey's already uncomfortably aroused state.

Caroline stamped her foot, then her eyes widened before she looked down at her foot in shock. "Look at what you're doing to me."

All he could think of at that moment was *Yeah, well, look at what you're doing to me.* And that made him laugh harder.

She shouted, "Just shut up!" then and stalked off toward either her room or dinner.

Watching her march away, it suddenly hit Trey. And

his laughter died a quick death. His heart all but stopped. His stomach rolled. But the condition of his body only strengthened.

He was in love with his son's mother.

And he'd never been in love before.

He had never known this wonderful, terrifying feeling called love with any woman, including Natalie. He'd sworn off anything but the most cursory of relationships since his marriage. He raked a hand through his hair, remembering Natalie's tears and the weeping sounds coming from their bedroom while he'd tried to study. He couldn't stand to think of Caroline in that kind of pain. He hadn't been able to stand it when he'd sat on opposite sides of a family court conference table.

They called it a "lightbulb moment." It was as if the mysteries of the universe opened themselves to him. Never in the history of the world had there been two more opposite women than Caroline and Natalie. Hadn't he been thinking earlier about how different Caroline was from her or any other woman he'd ever known? This wasn't about his marriage or any of the relationships he'd had or the women he'd known.

This was about him and Caroline and his love for her. It was about Jamie. And it was about what would make all three of them happy.

She'd said he had some thinking to do. But she'd had no idea how much. Or what about.

When his cell phone rang, Trey sighed and pulled it off his belt. It was the hospital.

Caroline put down the phone after calling for the rental car she'd had delivered earlier. She'd waited all day to talk to Trey about what had happened between them, but he'd never come home. The two suits had arrived that Marilyn sent over so Jamie would be dressed correctly for her party. She'd hung them on the inside of the front doorknob along with a note saying Jamie didn't wear wool because it was too scratchy. Trey's mother had begun calling at six and every fifteen minutes thereafter, demanding to know what time they'd be arriving. All of which meant Trey had not tried or had failed to "handle" his mother, as he'd promised.

She and Mrs. Ferry had made an executive decision after the third one to let the machine take the calls. The messages had gotten more impatient by the hour. Mrs. Ferry had left for her daughter-in-law's, and the rental car would be waiting at the curb by the time they got downstairs. The room had been restored to its previous pristine serenity with the exception of the video games she'd left for Jamie when he came to visit Trey.

She didn't worry so much about those visits now except where Trey's mother and his career were concerned. He had not been on duty last night yet he'd still been needed. And it was obvious that he hadn't kept his word about his mother, but perhaps he hadn't had the time. She'd cross that bridge if she got there. Were she to learn that Trey left Jamie with Mrs. Ferry too often or if Trey's mother upset Jamie, Caroline would *handle* Trey. That was all she could do.

Caroline really wanted to give Trey and Jamie a chance to be father and son. She'd never forget how touched he'd been by Jamie offhandedly calling him Daddy. Her problem was that she didn't know how to act around him, especially after what had happened between them on the terrace last night.

No man had ever made her feel what he did with just a look. She was out of her depth here. After experiencing his kiss, his touch, she knew she'd never keep her head above water. And worse, she didn't want to.

Her belief that romantic love turned people into twisted copies of their former selves scared her to death because she'd seen evidence of it all her life. And now she felt all those wild feelings and couldn't control them. She shook her head in consternation. To think that she had once chided Trey for trying to control *his* feelings. She wondered if he would ever learn the lesson she just had.

There was no such thing as control.

Not when you loved someone.

There was no denying it. She was wild, crazy in love with the one man in the world she should never have cared about beyond friendship. She and Trey had years as Jamie's parents ahead of them. The judge had sounded so wise that day she'd suggested treating theirs like the custody issue in a divorce.

The judge couldn't have guessed that the defendant would fall in love with the plaintiff, though. The dynamics between them had shifted radically since then, but she now saw that from the beginning theirs had been a different situation from a divorce.

In a divorce, the relationship between the adults who had once been united has become tarnished and broken. She and Trey had been strangers that day. Neither had broken the other's trust. Divorce was about negatives. She and Trey from the start had shared positives. They shared the love of a child and a determination to do what was best for him.

Jamie wasn't the typical child caught between two parents either. They'd shielded him from that. But there were other differences, too. The look in Jamie's eyes after he'd found them together had said it all. They hadn't scarred him. They'd accidentally given him hope for something she'd never even known he wanted and had never had. Two parents who lived together and took care of him—together.

So where could they go from here? Her love for Trey, though fragile, grew each day. She didn't think she'd survive the ending of a love affair between them, and Trey had made it clear that marriage wasn't in his future. She'd meant what she'd said about it, too. But she knew herself. For her making love meant being in love, falling more deeply in love, so that was a place to start her considerations.

It was a question that had haunted her as the hours mounted and Trey didn't show up. She'd wrestled with the idea of discreetly becoming his lover the way he'd all but begged her to. But in the end she knew that was wrong for her and wrong for Jamie. If Trey had loved her and asked for marriage instead of a few stolen moments, she realized she'd be more than tempted to abandon her long-held stance on love and marriage.

She still mistrusted the state of being in love and the institution of marriage, but because of the kind of man she'd come to know Trey was she might reconsider. But an affair? That, by its nature, had an end. Even if it didn't, they would be sneaking around, so she would wind up with the scraps of his time after his mother, his father, his son and his work. In whatever order Trey eventually placed the people in his life, she knew she would come in dead last. Caroline didn't mind being behind Jamie because Jamie's welfare came first with her, too, but she did mind playing second fiddle to the rest.

She shook her head and glanced at the clock. Nine-fifteen. "Come on, Jamie. It's time we left."

Wearing his pajamas and all ready for bed once they got home, Jamie climbed down off the stool at the breakfast bar. "Why can't we sleep here again. What about Daddy?" he asked, then glanced back at his half-finished log cabin he'd be leaving behind.

"He knows we might go ahead. He'll catch up to us at the manor," she said, then muttered to herself, "If there's anything left of him after the vultures are done."

She walked to the log cabin in progress and propped the letter she'd written him against it where she was sure he'd see it.

"What's that?" Jamie asked.

"Just a note to your father," she said.

She didn't add that the letter would probably affect the rest of his life. In the letter she'd told Trey she couldn't even consider an affair with him. She'd suggested they keep things between them platonic, saying she would be too uncomfortable otherwise. She'd also told him he had to make a decision between his demanding mother and Jamie. She'd said she understood his dedication to his work and trusted that he'd find a way to balance it when Jamie visited so that his weekends with his father would be more than a visit with Mrs. Ferry. She'd warned him, however, that she couldn't allow him to constantly expose Jamie to his mother unless he was willing to stand up to her on their son's behalf.

Caroline and Jamie arrived at Hopewell Manor tired, so she quickly tucked him in. Tempted to fall into bed herself, Caroline fought the urge and went back downstairs. Her mother greeted her in their cozy parlor with a cup of tea and a smile.

"So how was the Big Apple?" Juliana asked.

"Noisy. Energetic. Jamie surprised us both. Except for one major fright outside a museum, he did great. Oh, and the four-thousand-dollar lamp that got broken, plus I told you about Marilyn Guilford's evil little dog when we talked on Wednesday."

"Trey didn't say anything about something expensive getting broken when he called a while ago."

"It really doesn't seem to matter to him," she said, then realized what her mother had said. Trying not to show too much interest, she casually said, "He called?"

Juliana nodded. "To find out if you'd arrived safely."

Caroline wondered if he'd caved in and gone to his mother's and hated that she cared for his sake and not just Jamie's. But she did care. He had to deal with that woman, and the sooner the better. "Could you tell where he'd called from?"

"There wasn't any noise in the background I could identify. Why?"

She quickly explained about the cocktail party and the scene the day before between Trey's parents over weekend plans. Eyebrows arching high, her mother picked up the phone, pushed the phone-book-scroll button and reported, "He called from his apartment at ten-thirty, so I'd say he didn't go to his mother's. You're supposed to call him back, by the way."

"When I told him he needed to think, I meant that he should do it for more than the time it took him to walk home from Mt. Sinai."

"If you refused to call, I was to tell you he has some things to work out and that he'll be down eventually. It wouldn't hurt to let him know you got home safely."

She stood. "Actually it might. I'm not ready to talk to him. I might try to strangle him through the phone. Good night, Mama."

Juliana shook her head and lifted the phone again. She'd just let Trey know they were home. She smiled. And maybe figure out what had put the bloom in her daughter's cheeks at the very mention of Trey's phone call.

Chapter Twelve

Walking through the last tent, Caroline smiled and nodded to the artisans who were busy packing up after a successful weekend. Over a thousand people had passed through the winery and the festive tents dotting the landscape. The weather had been perfect. Low eighties, low humidity and bright sunshine.

Caroline's calf-length gauze skirt stirred in the breeze, brushing the back of her legs. The outfit's cheerful cerulean color reflected not only the cloudless sky but the mood of the attendees. On the surface it reflected her own, but that was only the surface.

Several shop owners from Hopetown had already called suggesting the vineyard make the arts festival an annual event. Caroline glanced down and picked up a copy of the gorgeous souvenir program and festival map Abby had put together. It had been so popular they'd sold all but a handful and had earned about a fifth of their proceeds with its sale. Caroline resisted the urge to skip down the lane with happiness. The festival had nearly reversed their financial straits. They'd moved within squeaking distance of the loan installment. If she could put off a few suppliers for a month or two, they'd make it. Just barely.

Until the next installment.

Caroline fingered the cell phone in her pocket, wanting to call Trey and tell him how much he'd helped them with his idea, but she hadn't heard from him in two weeks. Actually it had been two weeks, three days, one hour—she glanced at her watch—and twenty minutes. And, she admitted reluctantly as she loosened her grip on the cell phone, what she really wanted to do was feel his touch. He called Jamie every day, but he hadn't asked to talk to her. She could only assume he'd taken her letter to heart and had decided to keep their relationship platonic.

She tried not to feel disappointed about that. For the last two weeks she'd vacillated between being glad she'd written the letter and calling herself every kind of a fool.

A carved mirror she'd been admiring all weekend snared her attention, so she stopped to admire it once more as the wood-carver packed up his wonderful creations. Staring at her reflection and the evidence of little sleep that she knew lay beneath her artfully applied makeup, Caroline admitted the truth.

She missed Trey.

How he'd become so much a part of her life so

quickly was a mystery to her. Not understanding it, however, didn't make it untrue. Growing in her was a hunger for just the sound of his voice. She'd actually caught herself racing to beat Jamie to the phone one day earlier in the week, disappointed that her son had picked up an extension at the same time she had. Only her son's happily chirped greeting had saved her from looking like a fool, scrabbling for crumbs when she was starving. Caroline had stood in frozen horror knowing she'd have looked like an infatuated girl with a wild crush if anyone had seen her. Then, in the next split second, the sound of Trey's laugh had had her melting into a puddle of need and she'd almost overruled her pride.

Quietly as possible, with tears blurring her vision, she'd hung up the extension and crept back to her room to finish dressing for the busy day ahead. She'd spent the rest of the day distracted, having to force her mind to focus on planning what was quite possibly the most important day in the vineyard's history.

Sleeplessness wasn't helping matters, but the worst was the dreams, or rather their aftermath, once she finally did fall asleep. They were dreams whose promises were destined to remain unfulfilled. Dreams in which he came to her—a dream lover—in the dark of the night. Then, as if to mock her, he faded away all too soon. Each time he left, she woke aroused and needy. His name was always on her lips and his voice, whiskey-rough, echoed in her mind. And it stayed there. That wonderful sound of him breathing her name in passion—just as it had sounded in his rooftop garden when he'd all but begged her to come to him after Jamie fell asleep.

But she'd refused, slamming the door on future possibilities with her letter. *You did the right thing,* she told herself. Now if she could only stop cursing herself for her own stupid wisdom and him for listening to it.

As he took the exit off the interstate just north of Hopetown, Trey let his windows glide downward. Summer-tinged air flooded the car as he drove through the quaint, eclectic little town he'd come to love. The last time he'd arrived here unannounced he'd faced the unknown in a son he'd yet to meet and the woman who'd raised his child as her own. This time he had a son who called him Daddy and he was in love with that boy's beautiful, giving mother.

But different as this trip was from the first, there were new unknowns—scarier unknowns. He had a plan, and as long as he stuck with it…

Rounding the last bend in the road, Trey saw a banner stretched over the entrance to the vineyard's drive advertising that weekend's spring arts festival. He grinned. The festival was probably over, except maybe the breaking down, but if he'd forgotten about it, Jamie's constant excitement over the event would have reminded him.

His son seemed to be making progress by leaps and bounds. Every day they talked it seemed Jamie had an accomplishment to report, all of which had made not asking to talk to Caroline so much harder. These were some of the precious moments he longed to share with her, after all.

He hadn't wanted to lie to her even by omission, however. Until he had everything lined up the way he wanted it, he thought it was better to say nothing at all. And now he was ready, with the last piece of the puzzle having fallen into place only this afternoon. Gordon Severs and his fiancée had decided to buy Trey's apartment fully furnished with the exception of a few pieces he cared about, like his old bedroom set and his glass art piece.

Nerves jangling, Trey drove up the steep drive toward what he hoped was his future. He didn't encounter any cars leaving, but there were still several vans loading up in the Bella Villa's parking lot. He headed that way, hoping Caroline would still be there, circulating. It had been exactly two weeks, three days, one hour and twenty minutes since he'd last seen her. And he couldn't wait another second.

Trey found her standing at a wood-carver's booth, staring at an oval mirror. She had her hair pulled up in a loose knot with golden tendrils curling about her lovely face and graceful neck. She looked like a cameo come to life.

Drawn to her, Trey stepped behind her, wrapped his arms around Caroline's waist and kissed her behind the ear. "Wrap it up for the lady, will you?" he asked the vendor, his voice sounding husky even to his own ears. Caroline shivered and focused her eyes on his reflection in the mirror. She blinked as if trying to sort out his presence. But in seconds he saw what he'd hoped to find in her expression and grinned. She'd missed him. She was glad to see him.

"Trey, what on earth are you doing here…uh…doing?" she amended, looking down at his arm wrapped around her, then back up at him through the mirror.

He kissed that sensitive spot on her neck again, watching for her reaction, and was thrilled with the tiny shiver that went through her. "Buying you a gift." He let her go so he could fish out three crisp hundreds and hand them to the wood-carver. "Could you leave the mirror at Cliff Walk?" The carver nodded and Trey grinned. "Great. Thanks. Will you excuse us? I need to talk to the mother of my firstborn. We have some catching up to do."

"I have to help," she protested. "I can't just wander off."

He nodded as he led her away, her hand tucked firmly in his. "I know how you feel, but a wise and beautiful woman recently taught me a valuable lesson about keeping work in perspective. I have some news and I need to tell you before I see Jamie. It's important or I wouldn't drag you away. Please?"

Caro glanced up at him and smiled, shaking her head. "Okay. But only for a few minutes."

He looked around at the crews dismantling the tents and the vendors hauling leftover merchandise to their vans and pickups. "How did it go?" he asked as they walked up the outside steps to one of Bella Villa's balconies. He loved the view and ambience of the place from there. They'd managed to bring a corner of Italian wine country to the hills of Pennsylvania with the look and feel of all the buildings. Rows of thriving vines ran along the hillsides and a brick courtyard below was nearly covered with a vine-heavy arbor. He smiled when he realized the sounds of the mandolins and violins that floated on the breeze didn't come from strolling musicians but from discreetly hidden speakers. The mood was perfect for his proposal.

Romantic yet practical.

"Everyone thought it was a complete success," she was saying of the festival. "You could say a good time was had by all. Jamie especially. He may finally calm down."

"And the payment?"

"We're still short, but I can probably put off a few suppliers and run our credit cards up for the rest. The festival was a great idea and at least now we're within spitting distance of what we need."

"No. Don't do anything that could hurt that credit rating you've been working so hard to get straightened out. I sold the apartment. Since this is part of Jamie's future, too, I'd like to invest a little in it."

"I can't let you do that and I don't think my sisters and mother would agree. It's a family—" She stopped short, then frowned. "You sold your apartment? Why? I know it was impractical for Jamie, but you could have had some alterations done. You said it was perfect for you because of how convenient it was to work and the park. And you loved the view."

He shrugged, trying to look casual about it all when he felt anything but. This was the most important decision of his life. "It wasn't going to be convenient anymore," he explained and hitched a hip onto the balcony wall.

"You're changing hospitals?" Caroline asked as she sat against the angled top of the stucco wall. Shoulders thrown back, the heels of her hands braced behind her, she turned her face toward his, eyes narrowed.

Trey could see that quick mind of hers trying to work out what he was talking about as the sun dipped lower in the sky behind her. It was quite a sight and he had to fight a grin. If he played this right, kept control of the situation and his emotions, she'd be all his.

And he couldn't wait to get his hands on her. "I'm going to be working out of two hospitals soon," he told her, feeding her a little more of the plan.

She arched one of her perfect eyebrows. "You didn't learn much from that woman you mentioned earlier."

"Oh, but I did. You see, those hospitals will be Central Bucks Memorial and St. Stephen's. Both hospitals combined will only give me an estimated quarter the number of cases I usually handle in a week. So I figure that leaves a whole lot more time for a private life. I've already contacted Pennsylvania's state medical board. I've overnighted all my information and transcripts to them, so my license is in the works. And the chiefs of staff of both hospitals are anxious for me to put standby teams together and get to work opening up those trauma centers. My resignation's been accepted at Sinai and my last day is one month from today."

"You're serious," she said, her voice tentative. He couldn't tell if her shock was good or not. "Why?" she demanded. "Why did you do this?"

Trey tilted his head. "Truth?" he asked.

She huffed out an impatient breath. "No. I want you to lie. Of course I want the truth."

"After you and Jamie left…no even before that…I realized it when I was here, I saw what my career was costing me. I haven't been happy for a while but I didn't see a way off the treadmill. Then you came into my life. And when I brought you up for the week, I got part of one day with you—" Oops. Too focused on her. "You and *Jamie*," he quickly corrected.

She looked suspicious. "What about your mother?"

He let out a breath. "Then there was that scene with my mother. Pennsylvania is a lot more comfortable a distance from her." He grimaced, hating to talk about his mother at all, but she was a factor in his life. "I know you don't believe me but I *had* talked to her about how to behave with Jamie before she descended on you two that day. I had, in fact, told her not to come over at all. I've talked to her again in much stronger terms. She's not happy about this move, but it's time she makes a life for herself."

He wouldn't take the time to go into what he'd done before that last talk with her now. But he would tell her later. It hadn't been fun, but he'd talked it out with a friend of his—a therapist—and he was okay with what he'd learned. Marilyn Guilford was not now, nor had she ever been, what he needed in a mother. He could accept her for who she was and love her because she was his mother but he didn't have to like her—and he didn't like her very much. He was also under no obligation to live his life for her. He could feel sorry that she'd steered her life to where it was, but he could no longer accept the blame for it.

"Excuse me, but it sounds like you're running away."

"No. I don't think so. This is the first in a long list of changes in my mother's and my relationship. Changes that are long overdue but that I want to make." He shot her a quick grin. "So I'm not running away. I'd like to think of it as running toward someone." He levered himself up and stepped in front of her, his feet on either side of hers. Catching one of her springy curls between his thumb and forefinger, he enjoyed the hell out of the texture of the strands and the quickened beat of the pulse at the base of her throat. He leaned forward and whispered, "Toward you," against her lips. Then he laid his fingertips lightly against that intriguing pulse beat. "Don't even pretend you didn't know it was you. And you want me every bit as much as I want you."

Trey didn't give her even a moment to protest but covered her lips with his. He drew her full bottom lip between his teeth and felt the pulse under his fingers race faster. Her taste set his own pulse into an equal frenzy. Satisfied that he'd amply demonstrated their physical attraction to each other, he straightened and took her hand.

She shook her head and resisted when he tried to slide his hands around her waist. She put a trembling hand to her throat and shook her head. "I can't do this. Why did you listen to everything else I said that night and not that?"

"Because it was the only thing you said that was wrong. I don't take bad advice as a rule."

"But it wasn't wrong. If you don't think so, you're obviously a lot more sophisticated than I am."

He laughed. "Caroline, you're the classiest woman I've ever met other than your mother, and even she comes in second to you."

"Knowing how to walk, talk and dress has nothing to do with being able to sleep with a man one night and pretend it never happened the next morning. I'm not built that way. Physical intimacy is too meaningful for me to enter into it casually. But even so, I find I can take it or leave it as part of my life. I've chosen to leave it."

He took a step toward her. She retreated and dropped back against the wall again, surprised to find it there. Trey advanced and planted a hand on either side of her. "You want me to prove to you how hard that's going to be with me around?"

Her chin came up a notch. And her eyes hardened. "I didn't say easy. I said necessary. For me."

"Maybe you're necessary for me." Although he longed to tell her how much he loved her, he knew her distrust of that word and told himself that he *must* steer clear of describing his feelings for her on those terms.

He stepped back and took her hand. "Look, come over here. Sit down and let me map this out. I promise hands off. We'll have a completely logical discussion. I'm sorry I got pushy. It's just that I've spent the last two weeks wanting to have you in every way a man can have a woman and I'm a little overwhelmed to be with you. But I promise—" he held his hand up "—hands off."

She looked a bit distrustful, but she nodded and followed him to a table. He sat across from her, deciding that he'd be able to follow his plan better if she was out of reach.

"What did you mean? You want to map what out?" she demanded, her fingers tangling and untangling.

"A *life,* Caroline. A life for Jamie and me and you. A life where we share him equally."

"You want the judge to change our arrangement to joint custody?"

"No. Hang the judge. I want a life where we share each other equally, too. Look, we *are* attracted to each other. An understatement to be sure, but we do want each other. We've both agreed an affair would be a mess because of Jamie."

"We did? That isn't how it sounded a minute ago."

"My fault. I sort of lose focus around you. Stop me if I say something that isn't true, but otherwise let me get this out so I don't get distracted again. We're mutually attracted to each other, we genuinely like and respect each other, we have common goals for Jamie." He ticked each fact off on his fingers.

She nodded and he let out a careful breath. So far, so good.

"Studies show that couples who enter into marriage for love fail about fifty percent of the time," he continued. "That means if we were to marry for the reasons I just stated, we'd have a better-than-average chance to succeed because we wouldn't be cluttering up our lives with…what was the word you once used? Messy. That was it. We wouldn't be cluttering up our lives with messy emotions if we marry each other."

And his emotions *were* a mess. He couldn't argue with her assessment of what love did to people, Trey thought wryly. But he now realized that there were some messes that were worth any inconvenience. He just hoped he wouldn't scare her off. Looking at her stunned expression right then, Trey didn't think that would be a problem. As long as he wasn't around her too much, too soon.

Which was why this would be a very short trip to Hopetown. And why he'd leave her to arrange any kind of wedding she wanted and only return a day or so before the ceremony. That way no one would get the chance to figure out how crazy in love he was with her and let it slip.

All she had to do was say yes.

Chapter Thirteen

Caroline couldn't breathe. Truthfully she was afraid to breathe. Was this another dream? The sun on her face felt warm, real. The texture of the mosaic tabletop under her fingertips felt real enough, too. Her ears were the problem then. Surely she'd heard wrong. "What—what did you say?"

"I asked you to marry me."

So it wasn't her hearing playing tricks and she hadn't suddenly fallen down a rabbit hole. There sat Trey handing her the desire of her secret heart. But something was missing. Dare she trust him? He hadn't actually said he loved her—might he be going through all this just for Jamie's sake? It was ridiculous that those three little words he would not say meant so much to her.

"I don't know," she said instead, playing for time. Trying to jump-start her mind. She licked her lips and tasted him. He'd been practical about the logistics but not cold. She didn't know how she could have been so blind as to actually believe Natalie's lies. Nothing about Trey was cold.

Her pulse still thudded along at an alarming rate. She closed her eyes, then opened them and looked away from his compellingly handsome face. Unable to sit still or to think under his avid scrutiny, she stood. "I have things to handle that can't wait. Maybe you should go down to Cliff Walk and see Jamie. He's helping Abby strip the beds. I'm sure she can spare him. We'll talk later."

He stood, too. "Now who's running away?" he asked.

Trey reached for her then, and pride be damned, she backed away. If he touched her again, Caroline knew she'd give him whatever he wanted. But she had to consider this just as practically as he'd delivered the proposal. She didn't know if she should react with her heart when his proposal had been carefully calculated.

"I'm not running. I'm asking for a little time alone. I can't let this…this…whatever it is that pulls us together influence me. It could be fleeting. It could go away as soon as we give in to it."

He smirked. "Take it from me, it won't. It's too strong. Too powerful. You can't say you've ever felt anything like it before. I know I haven't."

"Will you stop? Of course I haven't felt anything like this before. I can't believe I feel it now! It's a disaster! How could you make me feel this way when you started off as an enemy?"

His smile this time was gentle and roped her in further than all the promise of fulfillment could. "You were never my enemy, Caro. I just misunderstood a few things for a while. All I had to see was the love you had for my child shining in your eyes and you became the most important woman in the world to me. Go. Take your time thinking. I'll go find Jamie and tell him I'm moving down here."

Okay, so he could still surprise her. "Even if I don't agree to…?"

A wicked smile flashed at her. "Yep. So keep in mind that I'll be around. All the time," he explained with deliberate care.

When had he gotten so close again, she wondered dully as his lips descended to her forehead and his arms pulled her against that deliciously hard body of his. Oh, how was she supposed to think with his scent filling her head? With his touch, where he dropped butterfly kisses all over her face, sending shivers through her? And with the press of his heat spreading warmth through the rest of her?

She thought she might be able to fight forcefulness and another outright sexual onslaught, but his tenderness nearly did her in. "You just don't play fair," Caroline muttered and turned her face so that the next kiss landed in her hair. It wasn't much help.

"But I play nice," he said in a quiet, deep tone that sent a shiver through her. Then he set her away as if sure he'd done all he could do to plead his case.

She turned away, trying to gather her wits, but they were floating somewhere out there among the vines.

"You'll know where to find me then," he said. "I have to leave tomorrow morning."

And when she looked around moments later, he was gone. Unable to fight the urge, she leaned over the balcony wall and watched him saunter along the brick pathway toward Cliff Walk. Caroline couldn't fight a helpless grin. She'd never thought she'd see up-tight Dr. Wesley Westerly III relaxed enough to actually saunter.

Caroline sank back into the chair she'd been sitting in when Trey turned her world upside down. Her duties had been a hollow excuse. She'd felt his nearness wearing her down. And she'd need to make this decision the way he'd presented all but one of the reasons for marriage. Being able to satisfy their hunger for each other had been too compelling a reason to ignore while experiencing the pangs of that hunger.

What was she going to do about Trey?

That had been the major question she'd been asking since the fifth of April, when he'd stormed into her office and made his startling announcement. Nearly three months. The question had changed in meaning often, but her head had never stopped spinning. Now that she knew she loved him, she wondered if it ever would.

Maybe thinking about Trey was the way to arrive at an answer to all her questions after all. Would she ever feel differently about him? Only time would answer that. But then she heard the echo of Jamie's laughter and stood to watch them by Trey's car as her would-be husband and lover pulled something out and put it on the hood of his car. She squinted. It looked like a toy of some kind and it seemed to delight her son. Their son.

Watching their delight in each other, she didn't think time would change her feelings. She loved Trey.

Which prompted what was probably the real question that needed asking—and answering. Could she marry the man she loved when he didn't love her?

Be logical, she ordered herself. If she said no, what would her future look like? They'd go on wanting each other, because she'd meant what she said about not having an affair. So they'd live with this horrible tension stretched between them. She'd done without giving in to her sexual side for many years. But Trey was a man with an obviously strong sex drive. He wouldn't wait forever. Thinking of the urgency she'd sensed in him when he'd had his hard body pressed against hers, she thought with a slight frown, he couldn't wait forever.

How would she feel the first time Jamie came home with tales of another woman sharing their afternoon? How would she handle calling his home early some morning and having another woman answer? She wouldn't handle it well, she replied honestly. Then there would be even more tension arcing between them but of a destructive variety. And Jamie would feel that. He was too perceptive not to. It wasn't a pretty picture, that future.

If she did marry him? Why marry him when he didn't love her? As he had, she ticked off the pros. They did like each other. They liked the same kinds of music and movies. He'd read nearly every bestseller she had in the last few years. They were even politically attuned. They were sinfully attracted to each other but both knew to act on it would be disaster outside a committed relationship because of Jamie.

They both loved their son. There was little doubt that

Trey had been a positive day-to-day influence on Jamie. His progress lately was proof of that. It was as if having Trey there had given Jamie the courage to attempt things he feared. Another pro was that sharing Jamie day in and day out with Trey would certainly make her life easier. Who knew, maybe they'd even have other children. And oh, now that she let herself think of it, she wanted more children. Trey's children.

In the final analysis, there was only the fact that he didn't love her that stopped her from seeking him out and saying yes. *Shouting* yes, she amended. When she thought of love from Trey's perspective, Caroline thought she understood what held him back. The women in Trey's life who'd been in it under the guise of love had treated him abominably. She would never act like either Marilyn or Natalie so there was every chance, given enough time, Trey would come to love her as she did him. There was little chance of that happening if another woman was in his bed.

All of which helped her decide.

She found Trey and Jamie in Cliff Walk's dayroom, feeding coins into an adorable iron bank. It was mechanical and entailed a puppy jumping through a hoop with a coin in its mouth. Once through the hoop, the dog dropped the coin into a bucket and then it fell into the bank. Each time the puppy did his trick, Jamie giggled, then fed it another coin out of a rapidly dwindling pile.

"Now there's an interesting concept. He gets to bankrupt all the adults and we don't even have the satisfaction of blowing off a little steam with the odd curse word."

Trey looked over his shoulder at her and laughed.

He's so happy. It struck her how much Trey's world had changed because of Jamie. When Trey held out his hand to her and pulled her down onto his knee, she knew the changes were because of her, too. That thought cemented her decision. "Which one of us gets to tell Jamie?"

His eyebrows arched higher on his forehead. "There's something to tell him?"

She nodded and he smiled, tightening his grip on her waist.

"First things first," Trey said, looking at Jamie. "Son, could you do Daddy a big favor? There's a box—" he held his hands up about ten inches apart "—about yo big on the front seat of my car. Could you bring it here?"

Jamie held up one stubby finger. "Wait. I got to know. Is it another present for me?"

Trey poked Jamie's stomach playfully. "No. It's for your mother."

Comically Jamie covered his heart. "Phew. That was close. I can only have one present a day unless it's Christmas or my birthday. Waitin' till tomorrow would've been reeeeally hard. Be right back. Don't go away, Mama. Daddy is reeeeally good at presents." He whirled and was gone.

"New rules?" Trey asked. "Did I create a monster?" She nodded. "I promise to work on it," he said, chagrined.

"Good. You're a good father already, Trey. You just have to fight the urge to overindulge everyone in your life."

His forehead crinkled in concern, he said, "I meant

to talk to you about the possibility of being a father again before you answered me."

He looked so serious. She was afraid for a moment that it had all been a dream destined to end as all her dreams of him had. Unfulfilled. She nodded, telling him to go ahead, because her throat was suddenly too dry to speak. Was he going to say Jamie was enough of a problem? After all, Trey had been raised by a woman who'd taught him that he'd been a burden.

Trey glanced down at her hand, then brought it to his lips and kissed it. "I can't see me changing my mind about marriage no matter what your answer is, but I'd be disappointed. Not being a father was one of my biggest disappointments with the divorce from Nat. I'd always wanted kids." He pursed his lips and took a deep breath. "I know life with Jamie hasn't been easy. I know you tell me not to feel guilty about passing SID to him, but I'd like to have other kids. I want to be there experiencing all the things I missed with Jamie. But now I know I could pass SID to them. If it's too much to take on after all you've—"

She silenced him with her fingertips, tempted to do it with a kiss. But they'd given Jamie quite a show once already. "I'm not your mother. Having more children was already in my pro column. I love your first child. How could I not want or love another one?"

He stared up at her. "So it's yes? To the whole package?"

Caroline nodded. "I hope we know what we're doing. Do you have any idea when you'd like this wedding to take place?"

"I have a month on my contract with Mt. Sinai. How

about you plan whatever kind of ceremony you want for July sixth? That's two days after my last day at Mt. Sinai. Just tell me what to wear. We can go for the license in the morning before I leave."

Was he serious? "A month?"

"Too long?" he asked, a wickedly sensual grin curving his lips as his hand burned a path up her back under her blouse. "Can't wait to have your wicked way with me?"

"I meant it isn't very long a time to plan a wedding." She tried to glare at him but it wasn't easy. Trey in a playful mood was hard to resist, she found. Her heart started pounding. Maybe a month wasn't a bad idea.

"You and your family planned a major arts festival in less time. Just invite the whole town—that ought to make it easier."

"Trey, about my family…. I'm not sure they should know we're doing this for practicality and—" She swallowed.

"Because we turn each other on?" he offered.

She nodded. "They'll be suspicious of your motives and—"

"They won't know there's a single practical reason. Okay. Our reasons are our own. I promise. Same goes for my family. Think you can pretend to be crazy in love with me?"

She wondered why he seemed a little sad. "I can do anything to make Jamie's life better. And having you in his life even part-time has done that. This'll be better."

"It's settled then. Before I leave I'll open a bank account to cover the wedding expenses and see that you get a credit and ATM card for it." He put his fingers over her lips to stifle her protest. "And since I'll soon be part of the family, I expect to become a minor investor in this winery. Pay the rest of the loan payment out of that account, too."

With his hand caressing her back, Caroline couldn't think, so she scooted off his lap and sat facing him on the ottoman. "Trey, I thought we talked about not indulging people—"

"Humor me on this and I promise no more indulging for a while."

"Now wait a minute!" Jamie grumbled in a long-suffering tone from the parlor doorway. "Do I have to take the box for Mama back to the car?"

Trey smiled at his son and waved him closer. "No, buddy. Come on over here and see what's inside."

Jamie handed her the velvet box. She looked at it uncertainly. Only one thing came in a box like this. "Go ahead and open it," Trey urged.

"Yeah, Mama. I want to see."

Caroline pulled the top open and Jamie said, "That's kind of pretty," but all she could do was gasp. On a bed of satin lay a platinum marquis-cut diamond-and-emerald necklace fashioned to resemble the new growth of a tree. There was a matching bracelet. She looked up at Trey and he held up a ring in a similar design. They must be worth a small fortune. "Trey, you shouldn't have. And I mean you *really* shouldn't have."

"Relax. I actually didn't. My great-great-grandfather did. They are called Aurora's emeralds, after the first bride who wore them. Since then, these have been given to the bride of the oldest son. She wears them as her own from her wedding day till their oldest son needs them for his bride. They symbolize the beginning of a new branch of the family tree. And this is the betrothal ring that goes with them."

He must have had some talk with his mother if she gave up these. "Your mother let you have these? For *me*?"

His cheeks reddened a bit. "Uh, no. My father had to sue her to get them back years ago. It was Danielle who made sure I had them to give to you." He took her hand again. "I've been imagining this on your finger. I'll take it to be sized," he started to explain but paused. There was no need. The gorgeous ring slid comfortably on her finger.

"What's *betrottal*?" Jamie asked, frowning at the odd word.

Trey chuckled. "Betrothal. It means engaged. Your mother and I are getting married so we can live together as a family."

Jamie's eyes widened and a grin split his face. "For real?"

"For real," she promised, and somehow Jamie jumped on both of them at once. Caroline swore to keep that moment in her heart and mind forever. She'd rarely seen Jamie quite that wildly happy.

He gasped and jumped to his feet. "Can I call Mrs. Ferry and tell her I'm getting my baby after all? She said I couldn't get one if you guys didn't get married."

Caroline felt her face flame and Trey laughed, pulling Jamie fully into his lap. "Give us a break, pal. Let Daddy get Mama down the aisle." It warmed her heart to see Jamie so readily accept his father's touch. Then he tore out of the room.

"Do you care if there isn't a traditional aisle? You know, like…not in a church? I thought maybe we'd use the grape arbor and have violins playing," Caroline asked after watching Jamie go off to spread the news.

"Sounds perfect. But I meant what I said—do it your way. It's your day." He grimaced. "I would like to invite my father and his family and of course my mother and Earl. And I apologize ahead of time for any unscheduled fireworks."

She tilted her head. "It's time to stop apologizing for two other adults."

"I know. And I also know that it was mostly Mother. Dad's a great guy. I swear I haven't seen him act like that since the divorce." He inclined his head toward the betrothal set she held in her hands. "And you can tell how great Danielle is. She could have insisted the emeralds go to my younger brother, Griffin. I actually think he'll be my best man. Let me know if you need another groomsman."

She smiled but was suddenly nervous. "Just give me a list of who to invite and I'll get the invitations out."

She had so much to think about. So much to plan. So much time ahead to regret her decision if she'd made the wrong one. She was marrying a man who hadn't actually said he loved her.

And Marilyn Guilford was going to be her mother-in-law.

What had she done? And how, after it had made Jamie so happy, could she even think of backing out?

Caroline heard a commotion headed their way. There was plenty of time for recriminations later. It was time to put on an act. At least for Trey it would be an act. He stood and pulled her into his arms as her family came in. Abby looked mildly shocked and Sam looked as if she'd swallowed a lemon but had been warned to be on her best behavior. Juliana and Will followed, carrying wine and glasses. Everyone was ready to celebrate Caroline's love match.

Chapter Fourteen

Trey parked in the turnaround in front of his mother's Hillsdale, Connecticut, home. He'd driven straight from Hopetown after he and Caroline took care of opening a bank account and getting their marriage license. He really didn't have time to visit his mother, but he knew he had to try talking to her. His mission was to make one last attempt at diplomatic damage control by telling his mother in person about his impending marriage. She was already upset about his move to be nearer to Jamie. Trey had no idea how she'd react to news of his marriage, especially if she realized he'd told his father before telling her.

As he rang the bell, he took a last opportunity to rehearse what he wanted to say. Which, Trey readily admitted, was a sad indictment on their relationship. It amazed him that he'd somehow kept himself from seeing all this for as long as he had. He guessed the important thing was that he finally had.

Trey did know one thing. He'd be horrified if he ever found out Jamie thought it was necessary to tread so lightly in conversations between the two of them.

He was lost in thought when a young woman he'd never met opened his mother's door. Why did anyone need three full-time employees to run a house for only two people?

"The missus doesn't accept solicitation, sir," the young woman said, eyeing him suspiciously.

"Wise of her. But I'm not selling anything." *Except perhaps peace,* he thought wryly.

She eyed his clothes. "If you've come with a delivery, you should go around back."

He was wearing his Hopetown Does It Slowly T-shirt and a pair of jeans. Trey grinned, doubting anyone had ever worn jeans in this house who wasn't a tradesman of some sort. "I'm Mrs. Guilford's son, Trey." He pointed to a picture on the hall console. "Of course, that was ten years ago."

She glanced at it, then back to him, but made no move to summon his mother. A guard dog might have been less of an obstruction. Trey thought this was a perfect illustration of the difference in the relationships he had with his parents. He never knocked at his father's door. He and Danielle would hand him his head if he ever acted as if their home wasn't his.

"Is my mother in?" he asked again, running out of patience.

She blinked, then got flustered. "Oh, I'm sorry. I'll

let her know you're here. You don't look like you'd even know her," she muttered as she turned and walked away, leaving him on the doorstep.

Shrugging at what he now considered a compliment, Trey stepped in and went into the day parlor that had a view of the foyer. Just as he went to sit on the pale blue antique sofa, he stood back up, remembering that he'd been rolling in the grass with Jamie. He looked around. Considering the state of his clothes, sitting down anywhere in this page-out-of-a-magazine room wasn't a good idea. Instead he leaned an elbow on the mantel and waited. Hopewell Manor, with its iron historic registry plaque and vaunted history and valuable antiques, was still friendly and cozy, unlike his mother's twenty-year-old touch-me-not house.

His mother came bustling into the room minutes later. She raised an eyebrow at his attire but didn't say anything about it, which surprised him. "This is an unexpected pleasure, dear. I thought you went down to see Jamie and look for a place to live." He could still hear annoyance in her voice, which he assumed was a subtle comment on his decision to move. His news wasn't going to make her happier, so he decided to get it over with.

"Actually I went to see both Caroline and Jamie. House hunting was never in the plans. I came straight here on my way back to Manhattan to give you some good news."

"You've changed your mind about moving?" Now she sounded hopeful. Entirely too hopeful for his liking.

Trey felt his jaw clench involuntarily. It occurred to

him that his mother used to exasperate him on a regular basis but lately that feeling had moved into the territory of annoyance. "No, I'm still moving to Hopetown. I rarely change my mind once I decide on something. I went there to tell Caroline about my decision."

"I imagine she wasn't too happy about that. She'll have to share Jamie with you on a more regular basis." Marilyn ran her fingers along the sofa table as if checking it for dust.

For some reason that really irritated Trey. "Mother, you honestly don't know Caroline at all. She was thrilled. Whatever makes Jamie happy is what she wants."

"Oh, I know that. She caters to his every whim. Mark my words, you're going to have a little hoodlum on your hands if you don't get him away from that woman." She shook her head. "The way that boy acted at the Guggenheim. I haven't been that embarrassed in years. And earlier—such a tantrum because Inky started barking, when it was the boy doing the chasing."

Trey counted to ten. "Did you read any of that book I sent you?"

"I didn't bother. I called Emmet Harrowgate. I asked him about this SID theory and he said it's junk science. You remember Emmet, dear. He's the new headmaster at Abraham Bishop."

Now he ground his teeth. "Mother, I don't care about Harrowgate's opinion or his precious academy. I trust the people Caroline has working with Jamie. She does discipline him. So do I. But she's also gotten him the help he needs. And he's happy. So happy." Trey smiled at the image of his son playing on the swing by the river.

"I wish I had been so…" Trey stopped, clearing his throat. "I've seen him make unquestionable progress since I've gotten to know him. I thank God Caro's been in his life all these years. She's a wonderful mother and I'm sure she's going to make a wonderful wife."

"She's getting married? But I've scarcely gotten to know him. Now there will be a stepfamily competing for his affections!"

It's always all about you, he thought but held his tongue. "You misunderstand. Caroline is marrying *me*."

His mother stared at him in silence for a full minute, then a sly smile tipped her lips. "How clever of you."

Trey had expected fireworks. Not congratulations. But what did she mean *clever?* For winning her? That made no sense. She seemed to hate Caroline. "Thank you," he said, still trying to puzzle out what she'd meant. "Caroline's made me very happy."

"I would think so. Gaining custody will be much easier if it's just a divorce issue."

"What are you talking about?" He stuck his hands in his pockets. "I'm marrying Caroline because I want to spend the rest of my life with her raising Jamie and any other children we might have."

"Have you lost your mind?" She stared at him open-mouthed. "She's a country bumpkin! The entire family are glorified farmers."

Okay. Now she'd edged past annoying and irritating all the way to infuriating. "Mother, Caroline's ancestor was Hopetown's founding father. Hopewell Manor is on the National Historic Register. The Hopewells are leaders in their community and are considered the cream of the local society—not that any of them care. Not that I care."

"And *I* don't care how well established her lineage is. Or how the other farmers and shopkeepers see them."

Trey pressed his lips together, trying to control his temper. "You seem to have misunderstood my reason for coming here. I didn't come for your opinion. A wedding invitation will arrive soon for you and Earl. The Hopewells have closed Cliff Walk for the weekend of the wedding so guests can stay there. I'd like you to attend." He paused. "But only if you work on your attitude toward my future wife and my son."

He pushed off the mantel and walked to the window to stare out at a rose garden, reaching for calm. The garden beyond the glass had won awards, but he doubted she spent any time in it at all. Trey turned back to face her, hands clenched in his pockets. She looked befuddled.

"The wedding will be July sixth. I suggest you read the book I gave you on SID so you don't upset Jamie and therefore everyone around him. This will be one of the most important days of my life and Caroline and Jamie's. I want us to enjoy it."

"A month? What kind of a wedding can I put together that quickly? And you haven't even started looking for a house. If I remember correctly, final settlement on a house takes quite a while in Pennsylvania. Trey, you just aren't thinking. For instance, that remark about more children. You can't risk it. You just can't! What if they're like Jamie? I couldn't handle two of them here. We'd all lose our minds."

He hadn't planned on unloading his childhood grievances on her, but her assumption that there shouldn't be other children pushed buttons she'd have been wise to leave alone. She was already rejecting his children as she had him. Suddenly hurting his mother's feelings mattered very little to him.

"There'll be other children if we can have them. And they may inherit SID from me just the way Jamie did. You could have had other children with Earl because they wouldn't have been a bit like me. But even knowing my children could be like Jamie, Caroline's willing to have and love my children no matter what. Her ability to accept me and my apparently faulty genes is just one of the reasons I love her so much."

His mother watched him intently, wearing an odd expression on her face. Then she stood and walked toward him. "You're in love with her? But…but this is so quick."

"I didn't know there was a time limit on falling in love. We've spent a lot of time talking and getting to know one another. That's months' worth of the occasional three- or four-hour dates I'd usually share with a woman, with none of the dating pretense. Give me some credit, Mother. I'm thirty-six years old. I know what I feel and I know my mind."

She held her hand out. "I'm so sorry I misunderstood. About why you misbehaved as a boy and about Caroline. I had no idea you were in love with her. That changes everything. I promise to be happy for you. Just don't forget your mother. I was here first, dear." She smiled a bit stiffly. "My goodness, more grandchildren. I suppose that will be…nice."

She took a deep breath and he eyed her skeptically.

That had been a suspiciously quick turnaround. Did she get it? Did she understand that she might have been there first but that Caroline and Jamie were his first priority from now on? Only time would tell. He hoped for his mother's sake that she did understand or she was in for a rude awakening. This was her last warning.

She took a deep breath and fussed with a bouquet on the console table by the window. "So. We have some plans to make. You're sure you want the wedding down there? You have so many friends at the hospital and it will be difficult to see to arrangements from this distance."

"Caroline's handling all the arrangements. I've given her a list of people to invite. She's the bride, remember."

Her eyebrows rose and she stiffened. "Of course I remember she's the bride. But all the arrangements? Well, I suppose I'll just call and offer my assistance then. No doubt she'll be overwhelmed."

Oh, no. She was not going to ride roughshod over his admittedly nervous bride. "You needn't bother. It shouldn't be overwhelming at all. Caroline and her family just arranged an arts festival that involved the whole town in less time than they have for this wedding. Bella Villa is a good-looking banquet facility and it's right there at the vineyard. We're holding the ceremony in a delightful courtyard they designed to look like a village square right out of the Tuscan countryside. Actually the entire property has that look."

"Have you given her a ring yet?"

No longer caring about the war between his parents or trying to keep an uneasy peace, Trey answered without hesitation. And it felt good. If his mother got upset, it was her problem. "I gave her the Aurora betrothal ring. Danielle messengered the set to me the minute she heard I intended to propose." Even in the middle of this tense discussion, Trey nearly chuckled remembering Jamie's confusion—*betrottal*. The kid was a character.

"So I'm the last to know, is that it?" his mother asked, stiff-lipped.

Trey realized that her mood didn't steal his joy one bit. Again he answered with uncharacteristic candor. "I should have listened to Dad and Danielle about Natalie, so I wanted his advice this time. Dad is something else I wanted to talk to you about. He and Danielle will be at the wedding. As will Griff, Susan and Rob. Dad will drive down with me early Friday. Danielle will be arriving Friday night with the rest of the family. You're welcome to stay at Cliff Walk, as I mentioned, but only if you can manage to be civil to all of them. They're my family, too."

"Good heavens, Trey. I'm not a complete barbarian. I assure you I can let any snide remarks any of them make roll right off my back."

Trey was more worried about her barbed little comments to them but didn't say so. She'd changed her tune about the marriage and had promised to behave. To expect any more would be pushing his luck.

Marilyn Guilford watched, seething with pent-up fury, as Trey pulled his car out of her drive on his way back to that exquisite apartment she'd had decorated for him. Steal her son, would she? That gold-digging Hopewell witch didn't have him to the altar yet!

She tilted her head, thinking—some might call it

scheming—but she was just looking after her own interests. After all, if she didn't, no one would. From an early age, if she didn't demand attention she was ignored. Her parents, so wrapped up in each other that they'd barely noticed their afterthought child, were never there unless she did something to catch their attention. Even in death they'd left more of their estate to Trey than to her. She'd managed to make him feel so guilty about it that he'd let her hire the decorator and direct the whole project. And now that perfect creation was gone. Sold.

Narrowing her eyes, she plotted. Maybe she'd let them get married without a hitch. Perhaps she'd even wait until Trey's adoption of Jamie went through so the boy had his name. By then all of Trey's capital would be tied up in a house, and if he hadn't seen how mismatched they were by then, she'd make sure he saw Caroline for what she was. He would have a stronger claim in court to Jamie by then. Maybe he'd feel the need to live far away from Caroline and then he and Jamie would have to move in with her and Earl. Not for long. Just long enough to remind Trey that his mother was the most important person in his life.

She grimaced.

It sounded lovely but it wouldn't do, unfortunately. That usurper, Caroline, could get herself pregnant before Trey wised up to her game.

No. Marilyn knew she'd have to move before the wedding. She tapped her fingers against her lips as she stared out across her garden, seeing none of its beauty.

What could she do?

And what would be the best timing?

* * *

Caroline stared at herself in the cheval mirror in the corner of her bedroom as her mother fastened the buttons at the back of the gown. Just after Trey proposed, knowing time was short, she'd stopped in Hopetown at the designer dress shop owned by a friend of her mother's. It had been a spur-of-the-moment visit on the off chance that she might find a suitable dress among the designer overruns that made the shop so popular.

Just unpacked, this Vera Wang strapless silk-satin wedding dress had called to her the moment she'd stepped inside the door. It had needed a bit of altering, but her mother was an excellent seamstress. Now it fit perfectly.

Perfectly. Everything was going so perfectly.

Caroline perversely wished something would go wrong. Lately this wedding had begun to feel like a runaway train. It refused to jump the track, and with each passing hour it took her nearer to sure calamity. Worse, it seemed to be gaining speed as July the sixth loomed ever closer. She didn't know how to stop it—or rather if she *should* stop it. Suppose she'd confused calamity with good fortune? Sometimes she just wanted to scream at the top of her lungs that it was all a lie. Other times the idea of calling a halt terrified her.

"Perfect," her mother whispered almost reverently, bringing Caroline out of her dark, confused thoughts.

The necklace Trey had given her now lay nestled against her collarbone as her mother fumbled with the antique clasp. Aurora's emeralds, he'd called them. Her heart ached with a sadness that brought tears to her eyes. Seeing that the tradition was upheld had been such an incredibly gracious thing for Danielle Westerly to do. And it made her feel more like a fraud than ever.

These were meant to be given in love, but Trey apparently did not love her. At least he'd never said so. Their shallow arrangement had reduced this symbol of a family's sentimental journey through time to merely an empty tradition.

"It's uncanny the way the pattern of the beading on the bodice and skirt matches those betrothal pieces," Juliana said, fussing with the train. "I can't help thinking it's a sign that this was meant to be. God works in such mysterious ways, Caro. Whoever would have thought you'd be marrying Jamie's real father when we all thought James was his father for so long? Or that the young man who stormed your office and took you to court would sweep you off your feet and love you so deeply."

Who indeed?

For three weeks Caroline had lived the way Trey once confided he had for years until Jamie came into his life. She'd put one foot in front of the other and had gone through the motions of planning a wedding and pretending to be happy. Pretending that her bundled nerves were all about the wedding ceremony and not the marriage to follow. Pretending that the man she loved loved her right back. When from the minute after it was all decided, doubts had begun to assail her. She'd silenced them at first, but a troubled conscience was hard to outrun.

What if he never came to love her?

What if he eventually found someone else?

How would she go on without him? After making love with him, wouldn't the loss of him be much, much worse?

But the answer kept coming back to one simple truth. If she didn't marry Trey, there'd be no chance at all that he would grow to love her instead of just wanting her. So she went on planning, hoping, worrying.

And once again she forced a smile. "It's perfect now, Mama. Thanks."

"I always wanted to make your wedding gown, but I'd never have had the time and I doubt I would have come up with a dress so perfect for you and that jewelry."

Abby breezed in and grinned. "Wait till Trey sees you. Caro, you look gorgeous. So why the worried look in your eyes? Still fretting about the arrangements?"

"There's so much to think of," she admitted, but arrangements weren't what was on her mind. The future was.

But, of course, Abby misunderstood. "I do this with brides all the time now. There is absolutely nothing we've forgotten. Has Trey decided what he and his brothers are wearing?"

"We talked last night. They decided on navy blazers and light khakis with silk ties instead of tuxes. It's less formal for a garden wedding, and they don't have to worry about getting together so Griff and Rob can rent one that looks like the one Trey owns. Apparently Griff's mother found pale-blue-and-cream-striped ties when she took them out for the jackets and pants, so that's handled."

"It's sweet that Trey asked his youngest brother to

be his groomsman," their mother put in as she fussed with the leaf-patterned tiara headpiece and tulle veil that went with the dress.

As tentative as her mood was, the memory of her conversation with Trey about Rob walking with Samantha made Caroline smile. She chuckled. "Trey thought Sam would be able to find a way to be nice to a twelve-year-old boy instead of one of his friends."

"I heard that," Sam called as her footsteps approached. "You can tell Trey for me," she went on and stuck her head in, "that he can stick—" Her hazel eyes widened. "Oh! Look at you! You look like an honest-to-God princess." The phone rang in the hall. "Be back in a minute." Sam whirled and was gone.

"Who was that and what do you think the pod people have done with our sister?" Abby teased. "Did she or did she not just say something utterly romantic?"

Caroline sighed inwardly. *Et tu, Brute,* she longed to call after her hard-boiled sister. Even Sam had stars in her eyes.

"Phone call for the bride," Sam called out as she re-entered the room carrying the cordless phone from the hall. "It's your future mother-in-law."

Reaching out for the phone, Caroline frowned, wondering what Marilyn could want. They'd had no communication whatsoever with the exception of the RSVP that she'd mailed back almost at the speed of sound. Caroline didn't want strained relations between her and Trey's mother complicating their already complicated marriage. So she forced a measure of geniality in her tone when she said, "Hello, Marilyn. This is Caroline. What can I do for you?"

"It's more what I can do for you. Trey mentioned that he'd left all the wedding arrangements up to you and, well, I've been thinking how unfair that is."

"Trey has approved every plan I've made," she replied, defensive now.

"Of course he did. Honestly sometimes that son of mine is such a man. I tried to raise him with some sensibilities but...oh, well. He's happy so long as he doesn't have to do any work. What I meant was that I don't think it's fair to you. So here's what I thought I'd do. I was planning to arrive late Friday with Earl. But I've had a brainstorm and it will give us the chance to get to know each other. I'm going to come down by train on Wednesday. My friend lives in West Chester. She's going to collect me at the Thirtieth Street station in Philadelphia and deliver me up to Cliff Walk. That way I can help with some of the last-minute details. Isn't that wonderful? I throw large affairs all the time. I can help you with everything you have left to do. I can write out place cards. Help wrap your gifts to the wedding guests. And there's the seating chart—you can't possibly know where to seat certain of Trey's guests."

"Really that isn't necessary. Trey and I—"

"But I insist, dear," Marilyn broke in. "I'm sure together we can fix any little glitches in your plans we come across. I'll see you then."

"No. But—" Caroline stared at the now-silent phone. She'd hung up. Disquiet stole over her soul. Nice as she'd been, Caroline just didn't trust that woman.

"Abby, do we have any vacancies at Cliff Walk on Wednesday? Trey's mother is coming in early."

"The gold room is open."

Caroline breathed a partial sigh of relief. "Well, at least she won't have to stay at the manor. What am I going to do with her?"

Sam smirked. "Take her sightseeing? Isn't that what she did with you and Jamie in New York?"

"Very funny. She wants to write out place cards. And wrap gifts." Caroline swallowed. "Am I supposed to be giving gifts to the wedding guests? I didn't see a thing in Emily Post about gifts."

"Some couples leave little tokens to remember the day by at each place setting, but it certainly isn't required. It's a little late to have anything personalized, so I wouldn't worry about it."

"How can I *not* worry?" Caroline wrung her hands. "Trey trusted me. What if his friends expect it?"

"I doubt they will. But if you're worried, we'll just look for something. What about the place cards she wants to write? I thought you'd decided not to do that."

"We had. In fact, that was one of the few things Trey suggested."

"Caro, calm down," her mother said. "This is *your* wedding. Yours and Trey's. He said he didn't care about the arrangements, but if he suggested letting guests find their own seats, tell Marilyn that. You have to begin as you intend to go on with this woman. I wish I'd told your grandmother to mind her own business the first time she dragged me shopping. This one is just like your grandmother. She'll walk all over you the same way you tell me she does with Trey if you let her."

Caroline nodded but she remembered Trey saying his mother seemed to only hear what she wanted to. She couldn't help but feel there was trouble on the horizon. Hadn't she already failed to get the woman to listen?

Chapter Fifteen

Just as the phone rang Trey dropped the last of the boxes for donation in the hall to be picked up in the morning. When he lifted the receiver, the caller ID identified the phone at Hopewell Manor. Hoping it was Caroline and anxious just to hear the sound of her voice, Trey pushed the talk button.

It was her but her voice shook when she said, "Trey, we need to talk."

A lump formed in his stomach. He hated being so far away when she sounded so upset. "What's wrong?"

"I think the optimum question here is what's right?"

He wanted to hold her. Tell her everything would be all right. Bridal jitters, he told himself, but asked, "Is it Jamie? Has something happened to him?"

"He's in bed but it's been a bad day. Your mother's upset him so often I've lost count—"

Trey raked a hand through his hair. "My mother? She wasn't supposed to get there before I did."

Caroline sighed—or had that been a sniffle? "She's been here since yesterday afternoon. She came to 'help' but she's created turmoil instead. I just don't see how you and I—"

"Wait a minute," he interrupted, afraid where that sentence was headed. "What did she do to upset Jamie?"

"She told him he's the only boy in the wedding not wearing a blue wool sports coat. So he insisted that he wanted to wear one. God, it's so hard to hear him say things like 'I just want to be a normal boy for you and Daddy' and 'Don't be ashamed of me.'"

Trey spat out a curse. He knew exactly what would have happened. "The wool touching him at the cuffs and collar set him off, right?"

"In the store. Trey, you promised to make sure she understood his limitations."

Now it was his turn to sigh. "I tried. I gave her the best of the books on SID and told her she had to read it."

"And Jamie hasn't been the only problem. She's been meddling and sticking pins in all of us for two days now. *This* will embarrass Trey. *That* just isn't done. We should be having a *formal* breakfast Sunday morning. More than the informal wine and cheese at the winery Friday night! I just can't do this. It's one thing for us to marry for practical reasons and…but I shouldn't have to deal with her veiled little insults, and neither should my family."

Trey thought he could hear a thread of hysteria in her voice. If only he were there, he could—

Caro's voice broke in on his thoughts. Now she sounded resolved, though no less angry. "Maybe we should thank her, though, because now I see that what she's been saying about the wedding arrangements is just a reflection of the real truth. I can't do it. *We* can't do it. I'm calling the wedding off. I'll tell everyone in the morning."

Trey felt as if a knife had been driven through his heart. She couldn't do this. "Caro, please calm down."

"No, I will not calm down!" she said. There was anger in her voice but he also heard tears. "This is going to hurt Jamie. Do you think I haven't thought this to death or that I'm doing it lightly? I'm sorry about the money that's been wasted. I'll find a way to pay you back. We'll just have to work on another way to share Jamie and to keep him from being any more hurt by this than necessary. Believe me, it would be a lot worse later when this fell apart and we wound up in divorce court. Please forgive me for not doing this earlier. I'm sorry if it embarrasses you. Good night, Trey."

The phone clicked and went silent—only emptiness at the other end of the line. And that was the perfect description of how he felt.

Empty.

Three hours later the better part of a bottle of single-malt scotch still hadn't filled that emptiness. But he was one determined man. And so he decided to ignore the knocking on his door both times he heard it.

"I'm telling you, Mr. Westerly, your son's here. I'd have seen him leave."

Trey found he couldn't really ignore the sound of Harry Washington's voice coming from inside the apartment but he gave it a good try by bottoming up his glass one more time.

"Thanks for letting me in." That sounded like his father's voice. "I'll see if my son's asleep. I promise to call if there's a problem."

"I'll be downstairs if you need me."

Trey closed his eyes at the sound of the terrace screen sliding aside. Discovered. Damn. Well, he'd just make the best of it. Drinking alone wasn't much fun anyway. "Dad. I'm working on a li'l project called getting drunk. Pull up a glass and join me in toasting the rest of my life."

Had he slurred his words? Hmm. Real progress. With renewed hope for the arrival of oblivion, Trey checked on the diminishing contents of the bottle of single-malt he'd set out to consume.

"Odd bachelor party with only the groom in attendance," his father commented offhandedly and settled across from him.

Trey filled his glass again. "I'm afraid the bachelor status'll remain depressingly intact despite my bess efforts. I am no longer betrottaled." He hooted at the private Jamieism, then continued. "Caro called off the wedding. Cheers," he said and lifted his glass, spilling a bit in the process. He should watch that now that he'd have to share his ticket to numbness.

"Why would Caroline call off the wedding?" His father was clearly horrified. Well, at least someone shared his opinion.

"Let's see. Mother's making a disaster of the wedding, and that showed Caroline that there wasn't any hope for us to be happy together. So I'm gettin' drunk. Bombed. Plowed. Three sheets to the wind." He lifted his glass again. "Here's to Mother. She always finds a way to get exactly what she wants." And then he drained the three fingers of scotch he hadn't spilled. "And apparently she wants me miserable."

Wes grabbed the bottle as Trey went to pour a refill. He frowned at his now-empty hand, then followed the bottle's progress to where his father set it on the ground. "Okay, you can pour if you want," he said and held out his empty glass.

"You've had enough," Wes said sternly. "If you're going to let the woman of your dreams go without a fight, you're going to feel bad enough tomorrow."

Trey flopped against the back of the chaise. The chaise where he'd almost made love to the woman who'd cut his heart out with a dull knife. "Fight? I don't want to fight with Caro. She was crying. I could tell. Never meant to hurt her. I only wanted to love her." He chuckled at the double entendre. "But that won't happen now. Nope. No lovin' for me. No fightin' for me either. I caused enough of that between you and Mother to break up your marriage. I'm just gonna stay alone. I've hurt enough people."

"Trey! Son, you had nothing to do with the end of our marriage."

"It's okay, Dad," Trey said, waving away the concern he heard in his father's voice. "Mother told me the day you left. I asked her why she made you go away and she said I'd done it, not her."

Wes Westerly looked about ready to chew nails. He

stood and stalked away, but then he strode back and settled in the chair again, this time as if getting comfortable for a long talk. That was okay. Trey hadn't had enough time listening to his father talk. "I had an affair, Trey," Wes began. "You know that. Later I saw a therapist to figure out why I'd done something so out of character. Let me tell you what I came to understand. I'd been telling Marilyn for years that I was unhappy with our relationship and that our fighting was making you miserable, too. She just wouldn't hear me. Down deep I knew the one thing she'd never tolerate was my attention on someone other than her. I finally slept with another woman. That got her attention.

"The only parts of that divorce I ever regretted was how I left and that I didn't keep fighting to have you with me."

"I missed you and Spirit," Trey confessed, feeling ten years old again and confined to a lonely dorm room at Abraham Bishop.

His father winced. "I fought as long as I could but I just didn't have your grandparents' resources. Then Marilyn married her lawyer's partner. I realized there was no way I could compete with free legal help. That's when I finally settled for what visitation I could get, and you know the rest. I never thought she would stoop so low as to blame you."

"Water under the bridge. Doesn't matter now." Trey waved a careless hand and extended the other for more scotch. He laughed, but even drunk he knew it sounded as if he was dying inside. Come to think of it, he was. "I can't think of a thing that does matter anymore except Jamie, and this is going to upset him no end. I know how he thinks. He'll blame himself."

His father sat forward and snatched the glass from his hand. "You're in love with Caroline. *That* matters."

Aware that he had to think harder to get the words out, he explained carefully, "But she doesn't love me. *That...that* matters most."

"I find that hard to believe. You said she was crying."

"Just felt bad for Jamie 'cause she called it off."

"If you didn't ask why she was crying, then you don't know for certain. Are you really going to lie down, get drunk and let your mother win?"

God! How could someone hurt like this and still be alive? "My fault. I let Mother fool me. I went to see her, hoping to keep the peace, but then I didn't care how angry she got. It seemed to work. She gave in. I should have known. I should have seen through her act."

"If you don't go to Hopetown and fight for the woman you love and the life you want, you'll be falling in line with your mother again. When is it going to end, Trey? If Caroline sounded hurt, then it's your mother who hurt her. If Jamie was upset, then she hurt him. Dammit, son, go defend your family!"

Trey stared at his father, trying to make sense of what he'd said. And then he understood and found himself blinking back tears. "They are my family, huh? I need her, Dad. I don't see how I can go on doing what I do if I don't have her to go home to. I lost a patient while she was here and it was so different. She was there for me and I knew I loved her."

"Then let's get you sobered up and get down there before she cancels your wedding." He lifted the bottle and eyed what was left. "You drink all this yourself?"

Trey nodded. "Uh-huh."

His father whistled. "I got to hand it to you, when you take on a project you don't kid around."

Trey swore a blue streak when the sun burst up over the trees and drilled a hole through his sunglasses and eyelids, then into his brain. Next to him he heard his father's strangled laughter. "You're getting a real kick out of this, aren't you?" he asked without opening his eyes.

"Oh, yeah. You have to admit this is part of your transition into manhood that I missed."

"Actually, no, you didn't. Last night was a first. And if your job was to impress upon me what a huge mistake it was, have no fear, I get it. I will never do this to myself again. How far are we and what time is it?"

"It's eight o'clock and we're four miles from the Hopetown exit. Maybe you should try to sit up and open your eyes."

Trey would be forever grateful that his father had forced him to see that he was giving up his future without a fight. And that he'd dragged him out of bed this morning, tucked him into his car and taken the wheel. Pushing himself up in the seat, Trey groaned and his head swam. "How long?" he asked, slitting his eyes and testing how good the UV protection of his shades really was.

His father chuckled. "Until we get there? Or until you feel as if you'll live?"

"The latter. I know we're about twenty minutes away."

"Then I'd say you'll feel like this until you can eat something and keep it down."

"That would be a novelty but I'm not sure I want to try that again. I may never drink another cup of coffee."

His father nodded toward the seat between them. "There's cold green tea and a bagel there for you. I picked them up at the turnpike rest stop while you were sleeping. Have you decided whether we should go to Cliff Walk or to Caroline's home?"

Trey reached for the chilled bottle sitting in the cup holder after checking his watch. "Everyone is usually over at the offices by now. I would think since Mother is at Cliff Walk, Caro would tell everyone there, then set about canceling whatever needed canceling from her office. I just hope she hasn't had time to do anything yet and that I can talk her into this again."

"If the woman loves you, it shouldn't be too hard to convince her."

"But she doesn't."

"That's the second time you've said that with pretty chilling certainty in your voice. And what's this about talking her into marriage *again?*"

"She has no faith in marriage and even less in love because of her father and some jerk she was engaged to years ago. I talked her into marriage by citing all the practical reasons we'd be able to build a good future to-gether. She's not indifferent to me, but attraction isn't love."

There was a long pause. Then his father asked, "But you love her?"

"Yes," Trey replied without hesitation.

His father grinned and shook his head. "If it wouldn't kill you, I'd suggest you shake your head to see if there are rocks or marbles in there."

"What's that supposed to mean?"

"I have every faith that Caroline will explain it. Is that the turnoff?" Wes asked, pointing ahead and to the left.

"That's it."

"Then let's go get this train back on track. And Trey, you might try telling Caroline how you feel. It couldn't make things worse."

Trey didn't comment. He was sure she didn't want to hear about his feelings. What she needed to know was that he *had* told his mother to amend her behavior. And that since she'd ignored him and upset her and Jamie, then she wouldn't be welcome in their lives. He just hoped it wasn't too late and that was enough.

Before the car stopped fully, Trey had his door open. He hurried to the front door and into the foyer, his father following. He heard Caroline's voice and rushed toward the parlor. She stood in front of the fireplace, her beautiful face in profile to him. Everyone in the room stared at her as if waiting for her to speak.

Then she did. "I have an announcement to make," she said. "I called Trey last night and I called off the wedding."

Everyone gasped. Everyone except his mother. She got an infuriatingly pleased little grin on her face before pressing her lips together, clearly trying to hide her delight.

"Mission accomplished, Mother?" Trey demanded. His voice cut through the thick silence in the room.

Caroline couldn't believe her ears. She whirled to face Trey, but he had eyes only for his mother. And they were absolutely glacial as he stood in the doorway with his arms akimbo. "You should have listened more closely. The marriage isn't off, the wedding is. At least, the one you've been trying to engineer."

That was news to Caroline, but watching Trey take on his mother so aggressively was too fascinating to interrupt.

"Engineer!" his mother shrilled. "This is the thanks I get for trying to save you embarrassment? Attacked by my own flesh and blood. How could you think I'd do anything to purposely ruin your happiness?"

"Because you've been doing it since the day you first noticed that I was getting too much of Dad's attention." Trey paused, a muscle in his jaw ticked, then he continued. "You sure as hell didn't care about my happiness when you told me your divorce was my fault. And what about the way you dragged Dad through the courts to keep me from seeing him on the weekends? Was that about my happiness or your revenge? And was clapping me in that prison, laughingly called an academy, supposed to make me happy?"

"I didn't know what else to do with you."

"Fine, I'll accept that the research on SID is new. But you've been told what to do as far as Jamie is concerned and you've not only refused to try, it looks to me as if you've gone out of your way to upset him. You've hurt that innocent little boy and his mother with your nasty mouth, and that I will not tolerate."

Marilyn huffed to her feet. "I don't have to stay here and listen to this."

If his eyes were glacial before, they now flashed hot as a laser. "No, you don't. In fact, I think it would be a very good idea if you went home and stayed there. Because I sure as hell don't want you within a country mile of my family. You're selfish and manipulative and better off out of our lives until—and I guess I've waited years to say this—until you know how to behave. Sound familiar? So if you ever expect to see me or your grandchildren again, you'd better figure out why you're so damned selfish. And you'd better change. You're through calling the shots and shooting barbs at me and mine. Juliana, would you please see that Mother gets to the train?"

Her mother nodded and Caroline watched in amazement as Trey stood aside and let Marilyn storm from the room. Then he turned toward her and held his hand out to her. "Caro, would you please come for a walk and talk this out with me?"

Caroline had never loved him more than she did at that moment. Maybe he *had* tried to rein in his mother before this. But today's scene was certainly far from the kid-gloved treatment he'd given her in New York. And now, having experienced Marilyn firsthand, she was amazed at how decisive he'd managed to be. She looked down at Trey's hand. Tempted beyond resistance, she placed her hand in his and he turned to lead her from the room. They were almost to the front door when Will charged into the foyer.

"Has anyone seen Jamie? He came to tell you breakfast was ready a good ten minutes ago."

Caroline felt instantly faint. "Could Jamie have heard me tell everyone the wedding's off? I was going to tell him later. Gently. I hadn't figured out how so I put it off. Oh, God, Trey. What have I done?"

Trey's arm went around her instantly. His solid strength felt as if that was all that held her up. Then he squeezed the hand he still held. "You didn't do anything wrong. You thought he was well away from the parlor. We'll find him. Can you think of anywhere he might go on the property?"

"I'll go have a look around the barrel room," Will said. "I've found him there several times."

"All the vineyard buildings should be checked, so I'll go with Will," Sam said and followed Will out the door. As their footsteps receded across the porch, Trey's father said, "I'll ferry the wicked witch of the Northeast to the train and get her out of your hair. I've barely had three minutes with Jamie and I don't know my way around your property. I'd be worthless as far as finding him. Someone want to give me directions to the station?"

"Our brochure has them on it," Abby said, crossing the foyer to the display of flyers. "I'll check Cliff Walk," she added. "Why don't you two look in all the places you've been with him?"

They looked at each other. Trey's expression was as blank as her mind.

"I'll check at the manor," her mother said from behind them. "He might have wanted his own room."

Stark terror cleared the blankness in Caroline's mind. "It's courting death to walk along the road. He's not allowed."

Juliana nodded. "Yes, but he might be too upset to be thinking about dos and don'ts. But there is the path through the woods. He'd still have to climb down the cliff across from the manor, but he knows how to get that far."

"He took me along that trail one day so I could see Hopewell Manor from up high," Trey said. "I don't think he'd try climbing down that cliff. The way he talked about how high we were, it must look like Mount Everest to him."

"But he might," Juliana warned.

Trey let go of Caroline's hands and took hold of her shoulders. His blue eyes deep with worry, he said, "Suppose you and I check the tennis courts on the way, and if we don't find him, we'll check the path." He let go of her and turned to Abby and her mother. "I have my cell phone. I'll call here if we find him. If anyone else finds him, call us." He grabbed a card out of his wallet and handed it to Abby, then snatched Caroline's hand. "Let's go, love. We'll find him. He hasn't had time to get far."

Caroline followed, nearly numb with fear. They passed the empty courts, then headed in the direction of the nature trails Sam had been cutting and marking through the dense woods on top of the cliffs. They all led toward the overlook to the manor but curved through the dense woodlands.

She wanted desperately to find Jamie but knew it meant explaining the reasons his parents couldn't be married. Knowing how much Jamie wanted them to be a family made it that much harder. She didn't want to make him unhappy, but she just couldn't marry a man who didn't love her—even if he did call her "love."

The realization of what he'd called her made Caroline stumble, but Trey's strong arms caught her. She looked up into Trey's beloved face and tried to remember what he'd said. If he'd really called her "love" or if she'd just heard what her troubled mind had needed to hear at that moment.

There was no time to ask or contemplate that because Trey froze in place and pulled her to a stop at his side. Then he turned his head suddenly. She looked around but saw nothing to indicate Jamie was near.

"What do you—"

"Shh. Listen," he whispered urgently.

Then she heard a faint sobbing sound echoing through the woods. Trey pulled out his phone and punched in Cliff Walk's number. "Found him. We'll be back when this is straightened out." He listened for a moment. "That's my hope.

"Can you tell which way?" he asked her.

Caroline, used to the woods from her childhood of playing there, pointed off to the left. It didn't take long to find Jamie in the ruins of a colonial cabin. All that was left was a stone fireplace with most of its chimney gone. A few logs had tumbled inside the stone foundation that marked the perimeter of the one-time home.

Jamie sat huddled in the fireplace, which accounted for the echo of his small hiccuping sobs. Caroline stepped inside the short stone walls. "Jamie, I'm sorry you're so disappointed but you can't run off like this. Everyone's frantic."

"It's all my fault. I wrecked everything. I hated those clothes and—"

"No," Trey said emphatically, apparently knowing full well where Jamie's mind had gone. He rushed across the ruin to the fireplace and scooped Jamie out and into his arms. "None of this was your fault. It was mine for letting your grandmother think for one minute that anything she could do would make me not want to marry your mama."

Jamie looked up at Trey. His blue eyes, so like his father's, were iridescent with tears as Trey settled on the foundation wall with Jamie in his lap. "Can I not like your mama?"

Trey's lips tipped up in a painful little grin. "Sure. I don't much like her myself. And I shouldn't have exposed you and your mother to her. We need to talk, son. First, none of anything that has gone wrong is your fault. Adults mess up their lives with no help at all from their kids. Do you understand that?"

"I got…" Jamie bit his lip. "I was bad at the store yesterday and then Mama said she wasn't getting married to you this morning and I thought…" Trey was shaking his head, which prompted Jamie to trail off.

"You have nothing to do with your mother's feelings toward me. She was willing to marry me even though she doesn't love me just because it would make you happy. But then she realized that would mean putting up with my mother." Trey sighed. "I've got to tell you, Jamie, I wouldn't have put up with her all these years if I had realized I didn't have to.

"What you have to understand is that your mother and I love you. I'll still move nearby even if we don't get married. I will always be your father and Caro will always be your mother. If either of you needs me, I'll be there. I love you and I love her. That will never change."

Caroline stared at Trey. So, okay, she hadn't imagined his words of love. And Trey continued to answer Jamie's questions as if he hadn't just set the world on a different axis with a three-word phrase. *I love her.* Had he said it for Jamie's sake? Her heart hammered. She didn't think so. He'd said it as if it were the most natural thing in the world for him to utter. As if it were a simple truth he'd grown accustomed to living with.

"Jamie," she said in a calm tone. She couldn't believe she could sound like that considering the foundations of her world were now as shaky as the one the two loves of her life were sitting upon. "Suppose you run back to Cliff Walk and tell everyone that you're sorry for scaring them and that you're much better now. Let them know your father and I will be right along for breakfast."

Trey's frown was more confusion than anything else. "Okay, buddy," he said, setting Jamie on the ground between them. Caroline bent and gave her son a hug, then sent him on his way.

"Did I say something wrong to Jamie? Is that why you interrupted?" Trey asked once Jamie was out of earshot.

"That depends. How long have you loved me?"

The stunned expression on Trey's face said it all. He hadn't known he'd admitted his feelings. He jumped to his feet and grabbed hold of her shoulders, desperation making his grasp a bit less gentle than usual. "I promise not to let my feelings for you complicate matters. I'll keep them under control. They don't have to affect you at all. We can still have a nice, smooth life. I promise not to let my mother or my love for you interfere. You know we're a great team. And you know you want me physically. Please. Reconsider canceling the wedding. We can make this marriage work."

Caroline knew then. The words were just tumbling out of him—uncontrolled and spontaneous. She pressed against his chest and he released her. Stepping back, she gnawed on her bottom lip, thinking how best to put him out of his misery but curious, too. "How long have you known?"

"I thought at first it was the night you let me unload about that young guy I lost in the operating room. But the more I look back, I think it started when I saw you in court and heard how you'd fought for my son's welfare. I saw how much you loved a child who wasn't yours biologically even though your road had been anything but easy because of his problems. And then I realized how much I wanted you physically even though we were in such an inappropriate place."

The idea that Trey had thought he needed to keep control of his emotions was perhaps the saddest thing she'd ever heard. He felt everything so deeply and instinctively. "Trey, this smooth, placid, unemotional life you've described is never going to happen. If it was just you fighting to keep your feelings in check, it might. But our lives are destined to be extremely messy because my love for you is going to be pouring out all over the place every day for the rest of our lives."

His eyes widened. "Did you just...? Are you saying...? God, what's wrong with me?" He snatched her into his arms and hugged her to him, then he took her face in unsteady hands. "There is no way in hell our wedding is canceled."

"No way in hell," she muttered, and they each sought the other's lips, sealing the promise.

* * *

The next morning the sun blazed overhead, but the shade of the arbor kept the guests cool. Bees buzzed among the vines overhead. Juliana sniffled. The fountain in the middle of the courtyard sang along with the string quartet that filled the air with music. And the scent of roses surrounded them as Trey watched his bride walk down a white carpet toward him.

Then, eyes only for Caro, Trey reached out as Jamie gamely escorted her to him and gave him his mother's hand. Trey made a private pledge at that moment to care for her in every way possible. From protecting her from harm to making sure she knew she was first, last and always the most important person in his life. It was wonderful to have found a woman he knew would never take advantage of that because she would care as deeply for him and his children as he did.

The ceremony was almost a blur after that, but Trey knew there was a video camera running so that was okay. He could watch these moments over and over and he knew he would, reliving each one. And then the minister told him he could kiss his bride and Trey wrapped her in his arms, bent his head and tasted eternal love.

Only the rousing cheer that went up and the quickened pace of the music reminded him that he had a little while yet to wait before he could claim his bride fully. So he sighed against her mouth and released her sweet lips. Her face in his hands, he whispered, "I love you, Mrs. Westerly."

A radiant smile from Caroline brightened the already shining day tenfold. "And I love you, Dr. Westerly," she whispered back.

They turned then on the urging of the minister to face a shower of rose petals as they ran down the carpeted aisle, then across the courtyard to one of the doorways into Bella Villa.

Constructed on the outside to look like a Tuscan village, the setting was more perfect than any of the guests realized. Because by tomorrow morning they'd be on their way to a real village in the Italian countryside and a private villa he'd rented for them. Seeing Caroline's expression when she found out about his surprise honeymoon was one more part of the day he anticipated. Not as much, though, as he did the night to come.

Trey and Caroline stood on the steps leading to the upper balcony of the banquet hall five long hours later. "Who are you tossing your bouquet to?" her new husband asked.

"I thought your sister, Susan. It'd be wasted on Sam or Abby."

"Susan has college to worry about. I say toss it to Sam."

She poked his chest. "You just want to pull her chain."

He grinned. "Hell, yes. But it's your call. I thought I'd toss the garter to your mother's godson."

"Niccolò Verdini? He's a complete stranger. I only invited him because he was going to be in the States for a race and Mama asked me to. Why try to hook him up with Sam?"

Trey stepped behind her and kissed her behind her ear as he chuckled, sending a shiver up her spine. "Because she can't stand him. It's a chance to pay her back for all the rotten things she said about me. And don't forget, he has to put the garter on her leg and not on that blond speedboat groupie he brought along. I know your mother despised *her* on sight. Come on. Let's yank a few chains."

She looked back at him and remembered her warning about Jamie having him wrapped around his little finger. She'd joined the same club. There was nothing she wouldn't do for Trey when he smiled. "You could tempt a saint. Okay, but you'd better protect me," she warned.

Trey surprised her by getting suddenly serious. He kissed her tenderly on the shoulder and whispered, "With my life, love. Forever and always."

She turned and stared up at him, transfixed by the tenderly fierce expression in his eyes, then the crinkles at the corners as he grinned again. "So go get her, tiger."

Caroline turned away and aimed her bouquet right at Samantha's ample chest. The ridges on the edges of the rose leaves caught the lace on Sam's dress, so the bouquet stuck there. Cheeks flaming, she had no choice but to put her hands around the satin-wrapped handle and snatch it free. Her hazel eyes shot daggers at Trey, as if she knew he'd put Caro up to it.

Caroline smiled up at Trey. "Uh-oh. Somebody's in trouble and it isn't me."

Trey grinned back and fired the garter at Niccolò Verdini like a rock from a slingshot. He, too, had no choice but to clasp his hand around the bit of fluff and lace clinging to his tie tack.

"Let's make a break for it," Trey said. "We'll catch the film when we get back." He pulled her to the top of the stairs.

"Where are we going?" she asked.

"To bed. If I have to wait another minute to get you alone, I'm going to embarrass both of us. Our bags are in my dad's car. We'll return it when we get back."

"What bags?"

"The ones your mother packed for you and my father packed for me when I was too drunk to stand up."

A car waited outside the entrance. Jamie and Trey's father waited there. She bent down and kissed her son goodbye, promising to see him in the morning. Jamie giggled.

It was his I've-got-a-secret giggle and was unmistakable. She sat in the car with her legs and dress hanging out so she'd be on his level. "Uh-oh. What do you know that I don't?"

Jamie covered his mouth, his eyes wide. Then his fingers curled into his palm and that little index finger of his bobbed to the time of his words. "It's a secret. If I tell you, it won't be one anymore. You know the rules, Mama." Then he jumped into her arms and said in a stage whisper, "Don't forget to bring home a baby sister."

"I'm afraid that takes nearly a year, buddy, but I promise we'll work on it," Trey said with a crooked grin as he lifted Jamie from her arms into his. "You be good for Grandmom and your aunts and have fun with your uncle Rob tomorrow. I'm counting on you to show him around. He's really interested in the vineyard."

Trey took the wheel after helping her stuff her gown into the close quarters of the convertible. With the top down, a Just Married sign fluttering in the wind and tin cans rattling behind them, they drove off the property.

She rested her hand over Trey's on the gearshift and tapped him on the shoulder with the other. "Where are we going?"

"The bridal suite at the airport Hilton."

She eyed him. "That hardly warrants Jamie's secret giggle."

He laughed. "Busted. We leave in the morning for two weeks in Italy."

"What? But what about Ja—" She stopped. *What about two glorious weeks alone with this hunk of a husband you just married?* She grinned. Lord but her face hurt from smiling so much. Then she remembered legalities. "What about my passport?"

"Everything you need is packed. Your mother and sisters handled it all."

"Good. Lucky for you Mama's father got ill and asked for her last year or I wouldn't have a passport at all."

He kissed her hand and sighed. "I'm just a lucky guy all around, aren't I?"

She squeezed his hand under hers. "And I'm a lucky gal."

Epilogue

Trey carried Caroline over the threshold of the bridal suite, which would have been an easier task without yards of slippery satin between the two of them. He laughed when he went to set her down and she slid from his grasp. But since that gave him an excuse to steady her by pulling her against him, neither of them seemed to mind.

It hit him then as for some reason it had not before. She was his now and he didn't need excuses to touch her. "Alone at last," he told her and claimed her lips as his. Sweet and vibrant, she melted against him.

"You know, some good did come of yesterday's turmoil," he said when they broke the kiss.

She smirked up at him. "You got over your hangover before the rehearsal dinner?"

"No, Mrs. Smarty-Pants. If my mother hadn't caused trouble, today would have been private torture for both of us. It would have spoiled the memories even after we'd told each other the truth. And we might both be standing here right now trying to hide how we feel about each other. We might be pretending this isn't special. Tonight wouldn't have been nearly as good without honesty."

"Hmm," she moaned against his neck. "So your mother actually brought us together. Really when you think about it, she did from the beginning. It was Marilyn who found the picture of Jamie. But I still think you could have done without the hangover her meddling this week caused."

"Worth it. Every minute of hell she's put me through was worth it if it got me right here, right now, feeling so loved by you and so in love with you."

He covered her lips with his and drank her in. When he came up for air, he had his hands full of satin and he wanted them full of her. "Is that dress going to take me as long to get off you as I think?"

Playfully Caroline whirled away from him and danced across the room. Her full skirt swirled and swayed. She was so incredibly beautiful. "Every single tiny button is a working one," she taunted, looking over her shoulder with her back to him. He started to sweat. But then she reached under her arm and pulled down a thin hidden zipper. "But when Mama did the alterations she took pity on you," she added, still looking over her shoulder. Then in the blink of an eye the dress slid to the floor in a puddle of shimmering satin. That left her standing in a strapless bra, panties and lacy stockings held up by sheer sorcery. When she stepped out of the dress, the three-inch heels she wore put the sexiest arch in her back he'd ever seen.

She turned to face him then and stole his breath. His wife had a body that was beyond his wildest dreams.

"And it's all mine," he growled and stripped out of his jacket, then went to work on his tie as he advanced across the room toward her. He framed her face with his hands—his none-too-steady hands—and stared into her eyes that had darkened to match Aurora's emeralds. "I love you so much. And I can't thank you enough for not letting me talk you into this before now. You helped make this night more special than I thought possible. I guess because you're mine and you'll always be mine—and now I'm sure of it."

Caroline didn't even try to hide the sly little smile his words provoked. "And you're mine and you always will be," she said, tracing one long nail down his chest, then slipped one after another of his pearly shirt buttons free. As she worked, she didn't look away from his fevered gaze—couldn't look away. Her fingers shook and her pulse thrummed just from the heated look in those laser-blue eyes of his.

Mission accomplished, she smiled more broadly and pushed the fabric of his shirt aside. Spreading her hands over his chest, Caroline threaded her fingers through the golden-blond hair she found sprinkled there. When she traced his flat nipple, she watched in amazement as it hardened beneath her fingertip.

Trey made a strangled sound and suddenly scooped her up in his arms. His lips descended, parting hers with his questing tongue. Tasting of tangy wine and creamy cake, his essence set her on fire. He moved with her to the bed and stripped back the comforter and blankets.

The bed was so cool it shocked her into a keener awareness of her surroundings, but then he was tearing at the rest of his clothes and all coherent thought fled. "You're so beautiful," she gasped when he came to her, relishing in the feel of his feverish skin, the rough texture of male chest hair against her breasts and his solid weight pressing her into the rapidly warming mattress.

"No, it's you who's beautiful. And the best part is your heart is every bit as lovely. Now what do you say we get down to the serious business of that little sister for Jamie?"

And who would have thought they'd get it right on the first try?

* * * * *

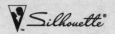

SPECIAL EDITION™

THE ROAD TO REUNION

by Gina Wilkins

Kyle Reeves vowed to keep a safe distance
from his longtime crush, but seeing
Molly Walker at his doorstep only intensified
the desire for her that he'd kept bottled up
for years. When Molly got injured, Kyle had
no choice but to return to the only home
he'd ever known and confront the woman
who stole his heart.

HOME AT LAST...

Available February 2006

Where love comes alive™

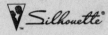

SPECIAL EDITION™

HUSBANDS AND OTHER STRANGERS

by
Marie Ferrarella

A boating accident left Gayle Elliott Conway with
amnesia and no recollection of the handsome
man who came to her rescue…her husband.
Convinced there was more to the story,
Taylor Conway set out for answers and a way
back into the heart of the woman he loved.

Available February 2006

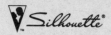

SPECIAL EDITION™

IT RUNS IN THE FAMILY

The second book in *USA TODAY* bestselling
author Patricia Kay's lighthearted miniseries

Callie's Corner Café:
It's where good friends meet...

Zoe Madison's fling with a rock star was ancient
history, until her daughter, Emma, flew to L.A.
to meet the star...and discovered he was her
father! Could Zoe protect Emma from her
newfound dad's empty Hollywood promises?
Maybe, with the help of a special man....

Available February 2006

You can also catch up with the
Callie's Corner Café gang in

A PERFECT LIFE, January 2006
SHE'S THE ONE, March 2006

Where love comes alive™

If you enjoyed what you just read,
then we've got an offer you can't resist!

Take 2 bestselling
love stories FREE!

Plus get a FREE surprise gift!

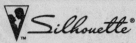

COMING NEXT MONTH